GLIMMER TRAIN STORIES

EDITORS
Susan Burmeister-Brown   Linda B. Swanson-Davies

CONSULTING EDITORS
Kimberly Bennett   Roz Wais
Chanda Wakefield

COPY EDITOR
Scott Stuart Allie

PROOFREADER
Rachel Penn

TYPESETTING & LAYOUT
Paul Morris

ADMINISTRATIVE ASSISTANT
Kaylin Elaine Dodge

COVER ARTIST
Jane Zwinger

STORY ILLUSTRATOR
Jon Leon

PUBLISHED QUARTERLY
in spring, summer, fall, and winter by **Glimmer Train Press, Inc.**
710 SW Madison Street, Suite 504, Portland, Oregon 97205-2900
Telephone: 503/221-0836   Facsimile: 503/221-0837
www.glimmertrain.com

PRINTED IN U.S.A.
Indexed in *The American Humanities Index.*

Glimmer Train (ISSN #1055-7520), registered in U.S. Patent and Trademark Office, is published quarterly, $32 per year in the U.S., by Glimmer Train Press, Inc., Suite 504, 710 SW Madison, Portland, OR 97205. Periodicals postage paid at Portland, OR, and additional mailing offices. POSTMASTER: Send address changes to Glimmer Train Press, Inc., Suite 504, 710 SW Madison, Portland, OR 97205.

ISSN # 1055-7520, **ISBN # 1-880966-42-5**, CPDA BIPAD # 79021

DISTRIBUTION: Bookstores can purchase *Glimmer Train Stories* through these distributors:
          Ingram Periodicals, 1226 Heil Quaker Blvd., LaVergne, TN 37086
          IPD, 674 Via de la Valle, #204, Solana Beach, CA 92075
          Peribo PTY Ltd., 58 Beaumont Rd., Mt. Kuring-Gai, NSW 2080, AUSTRALIA
          Ubiquity, 607 Degraw St., Brooklyn, NY 11217
SUBSCRIPTION SVCS: EBSCO, Faxon, Readmore, Turner Subscriptions, Blackwell's UK

Subscription rates: Order online (www.glimmertrain.com)
or by mail—one year, $32 within the U.S. (Visa/MC/check).
Airmail to Canada, $43; outside North America, $54.
Payable by Visa/MC or check for U.S. dollars drawn on a U.S. bank.

Attention established and emerging short-story writers: We pay $500 for first publication and onetime anthology rights. Visit our website for guidelines on submitting your work online.

Glimmer Train Press also offers **Writers Ask**—*nuts, bolts, and informed perspectives— a quarterly newsletter for the committed writer. One year, four issues, $20 within the U.S. ($26 beyond the U.S.), Visa, MC, or check to Glimmer Train Press, Inc., or order online at www.glimmertrain.com.*

*D*edication

This issue is dedicated to Erin Grace Swanson-Davies (Linda's daughter, Susan's niece), new college graduate and professional portrait photographer.

Congratulations and good luck to you!
We love you, Gracie.

Susan & Linda

CONTENTS

$\mathscr{C}$ONTENTS

L. B. Haas

A lot of dirt came early for me.
(With my father.)

L. B. Haas has had short stories in such journals as the *Hudson Review*, *Virginia Quarterly Review*, *North American Review*, *Antioch Review*, *Quarterly West*, *American Literary Review*, *Georgia Review*, *Western Humanities Review*, *Epoch*, *Cimarron Review*, and others.

L. B. HAAS

You'll Return Somewhere You've Been

When the llama guy and his wife split, they sold the acreage but left the llamas behind. Bitterness, we figured. A You-take-the-llamas/No-you-take-the-llamas proposition. Or maybe the scruffy-necked, giraffe-faced creatures had in their graceful dignity come to represent something—hope, happiness, dreams turned futile—something unbearable now for either spouse to look upon.

The new owners turned the animals out in the lower forty for the summer, a scrubby pasture half-sunk in the flood plain, and remodeled the barn for their college-age sons. It was understood that the llama guy would come get his llamas by September. But he didn't.

At twilight, I'd drive down the gravel road and find statue-still silhouettes grouped at the crest of the hill like a child's paper-doll chain—black-paper beasts stretching into the fading light. The first couple months it threw me. Ignited something—fear? anger?—in me. Nameless, faceless, an unsettling thing. The llamas clustered on the hill, their breath steaming out like clouds in the thin November air. I'd gun the engine to pass, spray some gravel, feel relieved to find beyond the hill the golden glow in my kitchen windows, sometimes the willowy flicker of Desiree as she moved from the sink to the table.

An elementary logic grounded me: the llama guy's situation was the llama guy's situation. Mine was mine. No overlap.

Kicking back later in my armchair, I'd be the Slipper King, the Hero of Hearthside Happy. While Desiree cleaned up after dinner, our boy Neil would show me the ship he was building, and the baby'd paw through my pockets for candy. Even doing absolutely nothing I'd know that my hand was as steady on our dreams, staying the course, as it was when I steered the Massey-Ferguson down through the rows. The new owners of the llama guy's property were not animal people. They'd never leave horses or goats behind. No shadowy creatures at twilight to spook you.

When a marriage ends, who is left to understand it? Certainly not the neighbors.

But the neighbors are still the neighbors. Prone out in these parts to doing neighborly things. Which means I had begun checking the llamas' water trough every couple days and dropping off a bale of alfalfa whenever I trucked one down to my own horses. Bare as the pasture had gotten, what with late autumn dormancy, they knew to look for me. Once I'd topped the ridge on the tractor, I'd find them pressed up against the fence, gazing expectantly in my direction. As I unlatched the gate, backed the tractor in, and began to unload, they'd stand aloof. Then the dominant male, this brutish shag-furred buck with silver belly hair, would amble forward, black shiny eyes watchful, and he'd lower his head to the bale, begin to eat. By some signal his female harem would know to approach after that. They'd tear strips of alfalfa away from the bale with their black-velvet lips, like children at a carnival unwrapping feathers of cotton candy from a paper cone. The young males would shift and stamp on the periphery, hungry eyes gazing at the bale, careful not to make eye contact with the buck. In some rough recess of their beings they could dream of that inevitable day when one of them would, in a display of chest-bumping, flared nostrils, and thumping hooves, topple the old fella.

Nature's intractable pecking order.

Except these were abandoned llamas.

Unlikely to be kept as a herd by anyone much longer.

God knew what would happen to them.

"They're dead meat," I said one evening to Desiree.

She looked up from the cloth she was batiking, the tjanting tool gleaming a warm brass in the firelight. "Not yet."

In our climate the simple fact is that livestock can't be left unattended in winter. Too unrelenting the wind, too bitter the cold, too persistent the predators: timber wolves, coyotes, sometimes dog packs. To leave animals in the field was to bring trouble down on you.

I looked at the stack of invoices and receipts on my lap, the month's work getting a leg up on me. The quiet in our house was so deep I could hear our grandfather clock ticking from down the hall. The baby was already asleep, and in about an hour I'd drive to town to pick Neil up at his First Communion class. I rustled the invoices, glanced over at Desiree. "The question is—when do I make the call?" I meant to the County Extension office, to report animal neglect.

"I'd call tomorrow. Beckett's not coming back."

True. We'd neither seen him nor heard from him since the day last spring when he up and left. The occasional e-mail went unanswered. The call to his university office got the standard Audix. No response. When I'd phoned the Animal Science department, I learned that the llamas were indeed *his* research property—*his* responsibility—not the university's.

Out-of-sight/out-of-mind animals may as well belong to anyone. Like me. But llamas were not in my future, no matter how much my son Neil had begged to keep them a couple months ago. We just didn't have the space. And eventually the new people on the hill would want to do something with that lower forty… Working as I did in town, it was enough for me to care for our horses and, in summer, manage the crops. I supplied pesticide-free grain to the Organic Pork Producers and during the off-season coordinated their mail-order division. Chops, bacon, nitrite-free hams: there was always a market for real food somewhere.

Electric wok at her side, Desiree was dipping the tjanting tool in the molten wax and drawing designs on the fabric stretched before her. Stars, planets, loopy shapes—and of course the Host and Chalice. This was a banner to celebrate Neil's First Communion. The planets all looked like Hosts, like a starfleet of Hosts orbiting in a churchy universe. Cosmic Communion, this. Wax bled into the fabric and she said, "They're predicting below-zero temps for the weekend."

"Hard freeze." The first step of an inexorable process that would culminate in January with biting winds, bright crystalline mornings. There'd come a long string of days when our horses wouldn't leave the stable. To stay warm, they'd roll in their own manure. Something in my chest snapped, and the words burst out. "I can't believe that guy."

"Believe it. Remember the hunting incident?" Desiree made a sound with her tongue. Instantly, the image of Beckett and his trophy buck wavered up for me out of some distant murk—Beckett, a 250-pound beefy guy, thick in the chest and broad of shoulder, dragging a 160-class whitetail behind his snowmobile. When he hit washboard, the carcass hopped up. When he hit powder, it sprayed a cloud of white. Animal Science? This guy? Whatever. Hunting season had ended two weeks before. He said he'd been target shooting in the woods. Accidentally hit the deer.

"Couldn't leave it lying. Couldn't leave it for the wolves."

His cheeks looked raw from the cold. The wind that day seemed to howl up out of a pit, as if chasing something. Each year after the thaw I'd walk the timbered part of my acreage and find the place where an animal had died, now just a nest of bones. You *could* just leave it. Yes, even for the wolves. Hungry as Nature was, especially in the lean and cold season, she'd find a way to dispense with it.

But I never pursued the matter with Beckett. Neighbors, you know. Snow fell that night, covering the blood trail of his snowmobile tracks—easy to forget about it all. Did he go on to mount the five-point buck as a trophy over his mantel? What business was it of mine? And so what? But in my mind's eye tonight, sitting here with Desiree, I could see the blood, and it was like that long ago snow had never fallen.

Brush poised over Neil's First Communion banner, Desiree nodded at me. "Scary."

"It won't be like that."

"How can you be sure—? The guy's a snake."

I stared down at the invoices and orders on my lap. Pepper hams, mesquite-smoked bacon, chops slow-cooked over apple wood. "My life is too full of meat."

"You want to get away."

"I'd like to live on the thirtieth floor of a Manhattan high-rise right about now. And not Manhattan, Kansas, either."

Desiree pushed her batiking away and came to me. Papers fell to the floor, a garden in pastel triplicate around us. She nestled on my lap. "No horses, no crops, no pork."

"No llamas."

With one finger she traced a thin line down my face, along my jaw, as if making a batik design. A light touch, delicate, with enough looping whorls that I could imagine an intricate world—perhaps a woodland expanse—of animals and Nature in balance.

Encouraged by her, I'd tried batiking. Once. Where she

created graceful scenes of multi-layered color, I globbed fat drops of go-nowhere wax on the fabric, exclamations of clumsiness. In my hands wax was dull and smeary, an inexpressive stickiness. But Desiree could fire it up under veils of red, orange, and yellow dye that appeared lit from within.

Neil had been a little quiet on the drive back from town, just sort of nodding when I pointed out certain crystal-clear constellations, not making any comments. I could see the fog of his breath on the window. Our parish had the reputation for being one of the more liberal ones around. Even so, the Catholic church *was* the Catholic church... First Communion-wise, I worried that the Transmutation business of turning ordinary wine into Christ's blood, for instance, might trip Neil up. As I'd waited outside his classroom door, I heard one of the kids ask the teacher, "But does it still smell like wine?"

Upstairs in his bedroom, Neil changed into jams, quiet. After brushing teeth, he slid between his flannel sheets and waited for me to tuck him in. He said, "What's a firstborn?"

I told him it was the oldest child, the first one born to a family.

He swallowed. Didn't have to say, *That's me.* "Will the Angel of Death come here?"

I patted him through the sheet. "Things don't happen like that any more. Those are stories from the past."

"But we still tell them."

"We *tell* them. We don't *live* them." What was my destination with this? A place of comfort and peacefulness that would allow sleep to come.

Neil was lying with the quilt drawn up to his chin, the very picture of cherubic coziness. But he kept meshing his fingers back and forth, kneading them in a nervous clasp. He had developed this habit lately of picking at the meat of his thumb, stripping some of the calloused skin away until it looked painful and raw. Once, he'd even drawn blood. His second-grade teacher sent a note home about it, inquiring about stress. She said the soreness interfered with his writing.

"What does 'mercy' mean?" Neil picked away at his thumb. "Like 'the Lord is kind of merciful'?"

I folded one of his hands in mine and smiled, remembering the ways he sometimes misheard things: *Our Father who works in heaven,* for example, in the Lord's Prayer, and *In eggshells so stale* for *In excelsius deo* in the Gloria. His hand lay in mine, quite warm, small, and still. An animal curled up in its lair. "The Lord is kind *and* merciful," I told him. At church, it was the cantor's responsorial psalm. "We're asking for God to treat us gently and with love."

"Why?"

"Because we need it."

"Because of the Angel of Death?"

Ah. Now I got it: firstborn, slaughtered lamb, blood on the door jamb, Angel of Death passing over. "Because all of God's creatures live on a planet harsh enough—the only inhabited one in this galaxy—that we have to pray for mercy just to help us through our day."

"It stinks."

"You'd do things differently."

Neil became animated, even rising up on an elbow. "No sickness. No people without food. No bullies. But fireworks still, and mountains." His eyes widened, seeing it there in the space between us. "Waterfalls, too. No bees. Or wasps. But rainbows. Also fishing holes and fountains."

"Mmmm. I want to visit *your* world."

"And stay?"

"For a while."

"But you'd come back? *Here*—?"

"I think so." Neil had begun meshing his fingers again, back and forth, back and forth. "But maybe not," I said quickly. I played my hand in among his, a creature cozying in. "Maybe I'd just stay."

"Dad, what's going to happen to the llamas?"

It surprised me. Other than pestering me to keep them a couple months back, he'd not mentioned them again. "They'll have to go somewhere else to live."

"Will God be kind of merciful?"

Again, I smiled—but right away I felt something sad in it. The fact that he'd spoken of Beckett's llamas and the Angel of Death practically in the same breath—that didn't sit well with me. Didn't bode well for peaceful slumber, either. Mine, not his. "They're out of God's hands."

"But he's got the whole *world* in His hands. Even the little tiny babies." Neil yanked the flannel sheet tightly around him, cocoon-like—a ritual of protection each night. He claimed it kept him safe in the dark.

"*We're* in His hands. Our world is. But He gives us some things to decide about. The llamas are in Beckett's hands. *He's* the god of that world."

"Can't you help?" He screwed up his face—Serious & Somber Neil—and his eyes looked spacious, almost alarmed, as if dilating with his own private Armageddon. Biblical evil, I thought. How dare they teach this stuff to children? God, I sometimes hated the church.

"I *hope* I can help," I told Neil.

"It stinks."

I clasped him to me. Bony ribs, little-boy shoulders, kissably smooth cheeks. Couldn't it all be this simple and real?

And just like that, a moment later, everything was normal and forgotten, the routine of bedtime starting to kick in. I patted his leg through the sheet and listened to him: *Now I lay me down to sleep...* But cold had sunk like stone in my gut. So inadequate, I thought, the things that get us through the night—prayers, kisses, fuzzy sheets wrapped tight.

The next morning I phoned the sheriff, made an official report of animal abandonment. The voice I spoke to on the other end of the line remarked that there was a lot of that just now, what with the change of season, stock left unattended. A week or so went by, the bitter cold arriving predictably as the forecasters had said. As far as I could tell, nobody had come to check on the animals. No sign of Beckett, either.

Sitting in my office downtown, I found myself picking at the callous on my thumb one day—picking, picking.

When the new people moved in last summer, I took them a ten-pound ham, sugar cured and slow smoked over hickory, our best seller, the one that always flew out of stock each Christmas and Easter. The guy was a slope-shouldered fellow a little older than me with frame glasses and a razor-trimmed moustache going grey. He wore a T-shirt and a pair of nylon running shorts. A cell phone was clipped to his waistband. His wife was hard-coiffed—for some reason I thought of Margaret Thatcher—with hatch-mark worry lines to either side of the eye. Appropriate on a woman who had raised teenage sons. I shook hands with them both and found in that quick clasp a softness of palm that spoke to me of too many hours spent seated before a computer terminal, too long an online-all-the-time lifestyle. Turned out neither had ever lived away from the city. This seven-plus-forty was a first for them. An investment. They didn't even have a tractor yet. And, like I said, not animal people.

Margaret Thatcher looked at him. "Maybe we should call the realtor." This after I'd mentioned the llamas. What the hell was a realtor going to do? Once they'd closed the deal, realtors tended to disappear.

Cell Phone tapped his Nokia 5120. "Got her on speed dial still."

She turned back to me, a severe-looking woman with deep smile lines etched to either side of her mouth, as if with a stylus. Smile lines. Right. It didn't look like she ever smiled. Her scent reminded me of department-store perfume counters—an expensive flower essence. Past her shoulder, I could see his 'n' her golf carts parked inside the barn. One had a canopy of pale blue fringe, the other a canopy of pink. The fringe undulated in the slight breeze. I glanced from the golf carts to her.

Cell Phone said, "From what I understand it was a real doozy, their divorce."

I nodded.

She was cradling the nitrite-free ham in her arms like a baby. The sight would have made a perfect photo in the weird Diane Arbus style. "Llamas weren't all they left behind."

I leaned in. "How's that?"

"Hon, don't bother the guy. He was their *neighbor*." Cell Phone looked at me. "I'm sure he got an earful."

All at once, Margaret Thatcher blurted, "You can tell there was a lot of hate in that house." Her face went white, her eyes wide. The instant she said it I knew she wanted those words back.

Her husband turned. "You don't mean the accordion."

"Ugh." She turned back to me, the seasoned diplomat catching herself now. In an instant she'd composed her face. I had no idea what she did for a living, but if the public were involved I could see how cool, controlling clarity might figure in. She said, "Now how long did you say you've lived out here?"

I shaded my eyes in Cell Phone's direction. "I never heard accordion music around here."

He snorted. "Thing wasn't for playing. Busting up is more like it. Had a pitchfork clear through the bellows. Hurled like a lightning bolt."

"Oh, God." His wife shifted the ham to the hollow of her other arm, looked down at it. This was the sobering instant— full of regret and self-loathing—just after Diane Arbus has snapped the pix.

T. LEON 02

"Can you believe he left it there? Sitting? First thing we saw when we climbed the hay loft." Cell Phone jutted his chin in the direction of the barn. "The realtor didn't even know it was there." Indignation was thick in his voice.

A phone chirped, and I assumed it was his. He must have too, because he was right on it, scooping it from his waistband in one practiced move. It had a faceplate of golf scenes. He teethed the antenna up. Turned out, it was Margaret Thatcher's cell phone. Smoked ham slung in the balance of one arm, she slid a slim candy-apple-red model out of her hip pocket and wandered over toward the barn, giving her attention to the voice on the line. He clipped his phone to his waistband again. Neil had been at me to buy one of these, said it would come in handy on the farm, said Mom could use it, I could take it to work, everything. I guess one of his friends from church—the dad—had one.

Cell Phone scruffed his hand through his hair, eyed me. "So you see, llamas aren't the whole story." His wife was standing just inside the barn now, and he looked over at her. She had set the ham down in the passenger seat of the pink golf cart and had begun to lean against it, absentmindedly chatting away. Another Diane Arbus moment. Cell Phone shook his head. "Maybe any married stiff wonders... An ugly divorce. Desperation. Is it a There-but-for-the-grace-of-God-go-I situation? You know? Can you put yourself in *his* shoes?" He chucked me on the arm. "You're a married stiff, right? Damn near gives you the willies, huh?"

I said nothing but remembered how those left-behind llamas spooked me, how relieved I always felt to crest their dark hill and find the golden glow in my windows.

Cell Phone huffed his breath out in one choppy stream. "Quite frankly, we'd like to be done with this shit. *Their* shit. For the money we're paying out here."

I didn't blame the guy. Accordions, pitchforks, and llamas. What a lousy mix. Like items on an aptitude test, where the point is to make a logical connection between three seemingly unrelated things. An indication of intelligence. You could be smart and not want to figure this out.

When I left that day, I noticed they'd piled stuff out by the road, waiting for trash pickup. It would be a couple weeks still before they figured out that there was no trash pickup out here. *You* were your trash pickup, you and a rust-bucket truck. Enough to cause idyllic dreams of a country acreage to go sour, whether you both had golf carts or not. I glanced through the stuff they'd piled up, found a gearbox from an old John Deere I thought I could salvage and, of course, the pitchfork. I took them both with me, stuck the gearbox in my shed for later, and left the pitchfork down at the lower forty with the llamas. For when I needed to unload a bale. Didn't see the accordion, though, in their pile of stuff, mutilated or not.

The Saturday after I'd reported Beckett to the authorities I was sitting at the dining table at dawn, shaking off sleep and sipping some coffee. A light powdery snow had sifted down overnight, just enough to lend a luminous wintry feel to this otherwise grey sunrise. The sky promised more snow—four or five inches, they were saying. No one else was up yet.

The coffee mug felt warm against the heel of my hand, and I sat listening in the dawn stillness to the ticking of the clock. With the sunrise had come the wind. It whipped the light snow, drove flakes pinging against the windows, a counter cadence to the clock.

Then I heard the shot.

A clipped clear report on the morning air. It carried like the sound of breaking glass. My head jerked toward the south windows. I turned just in time to catch a whole flock of crows lifting up out of a stubble field, black smudges on the paper sky.

In the mud room I stumbled into my boots and then pushed out into the wind, still pulling my Carhartt on. Bare tree limbs clicked against each other, a nervous sort of switching. My boots crunched in the powdery stuff. The ground still felt soft and friable underfoot, the hard freeze not gripping it yet. From the stable, my horses nickered as I passed. Their trough was topped off with a windowpane of ice. I smashed it through and kept going.

At the top of the hill it was gustier, a cutting sort of brisk wind that sliced through the quilted lining of my coat. My eyes teared up, and I stood for a few moments blinking. Then

L. B. HAAS

I saw it—blood on the snow. Stark. Dramatic. Primal. The llama struggling to rise up on all fours. Silver belly-fur stiff with blood.

I scanned the scene, taking it in panoramically. Trough. Trees. Scrubby weeds gone dormant. The alfalfa bale I left last week. Everything was normal... but it was not normal.

The rest of the herd had clustered at the farthest edge of the lower forty, a dipped-out basin that stood under water all summer. It was a sheet of brittle ice today. Their hooves had shattered through. The gutshot llama was struggling to join his herd.

And there he was—Beckett.

Twelve gauge in hand, he was looking not at the llamas but down at the snow around his feet. He was wearing a thin terry-cloth bathrobe over a pair of sweatpants—no shirt— and the robe was flowing open so that I could see his bare chest. The skin there looked raw from the cold and wind. He was toeing something in the snow at his feet, his pair of worn leather house slippers dark with wetness. He crouched down, the bathrobe flaring out behind him like a banner, and he began pawing at something in the tufts of grass. Like a mad king, I thought. Crowned with bed-head. Wiry strands of greying hair stood stiffly straight, defying the wind.

The world was in Beckett's hands. Along with a shotgun.

I could not leave the world in Beckett's hands.

"Yo!"

He straightened laboriously, his reactions a little slow. Drunk, I thought. Along the periphery of my vision I saw the wounded llama hobbling toward its herd, dropping its hind-quarters, then staggering up again. Beckett squinted in my direction, eyes adjusting to the distance. I hadn't seen the guy since last spring. It was like he'd put on ten years since then. Face haggard, skin coarse looking, belly sagging over the waistband of his sweat pants, a real load of cheese there.

"Beckett, what's going on?"

"Lost a contact," he yelled. He jutted the rifle's barrel sharply skyward. It was a twin bore up-and-under. "Thing's got more kick than I remember."

"You need some help, Beckett? Here. Let me hold that for you." Close now, I held my hand out, gestured toward the shotgun.

He grinned, squeezed one eye shut—the one without the contact? A laugh wheezed from between his lips, its own eerie wind. "Stay back, man."

My heart thumped wildly, adrenaline and early-morning caffeine amplifying each other. The thought of Desiree, Neil, and the baby sleeping peacefully in their beds came to me, two vastly different worlds existing side by side. What the hell was I *doing*?

"That llama's been shot. Let's put it out of its misery." Elementary logic. Simple, reassuring. The need not to blame Beckett, or name him as the agent here, uppermost. That old pitchfork still leaned against the gate where I'd left it, its tines jammed down in the near-frozen ground. I jerked it up. Cell phone, I thought. What I needed was a cell phone right now so I could call the sheriff. But all I had was this.

Beckett glared at me, lip curled. "Put it out of its misery? With *that*, bub? Then you're a more heartless bastard than I." He spat in the snow, glanced at the gutshot llama, his eyes restless, darting about, something flushed out of cover. He smelled powerfully of a sour-mash whiskey, an astringent, almost kerosene-like odor that carried on the snowy air. The wheels were turning behind Beckett's eyes. Ideas forming. I didn't want Beckett getting ideas.

All at once, he leveled the gun barrel at me, almost casual-like. "Maybe I should put *you* out of *your* misery."

"But I'm not miserable." Elementary. Simple. Declarative. Befitting a second-grade reader. The Lord is kind of merciful.

"Maybe I should just put myself out of misery." He tipped the gun barrel up under his chin. It was an easy motion. The thing fit quite naturally there. It bit into a loose flap of skin just beneath. I doubted it was the first time he'd done such a thing.

"Not worth it, Beckett."

"Fuck-around whore. Screwing somebody. Out here even, from what I hear tell." He arched his eyebrows. "Wasn't you, was it?"

"I know how to stay on my side of the fence."

"You're on my property now, bub."

"Think again, Beckett." I inclined my head toward the house on the hill. The new guy.

He snorted, spat, brought the rifle back to hang loosely at his side. When he did, I heard something click in the pocket of his bathrobe. Too small to be car keys. More like extra shells for the shotgun rattling against each other. "Idiot bastard," Beckett said. "Paying California prices for something that's not even in California."

I held the pitchfork out. "You lost something." Diversionary Tactics 101.

He didn't look at it, but at me, January's ice in his gaze. "What do you know about it?"

I shook the thing in my bare hand. "Come on, Beckett. You left stuff behind."

He did look at the pitchfork then. "Ah! So *that's* where it is. I wondered what happened. Figured The Bitch took it. Why, I was saying the other day—who's got my goddamn pitchfork?" He rubbed his foot through the snow at his feet once more, as if remembering the lost contact lens. When he looked up, he fixed me with a cold stare. "You called The Man on me."

"Had to, Beckett. You weren't taking care. You've got to take care of what's yours."

"Well, that's why I'm here." Suddenly, he swung around, rifle at his hip. Fast. Like a mechanism that surged more powerfully into motion than you'd thought possible: jet planes, steam shovels, hydraulic equipment. He pointed the barrel toward the herd, squeezed off a no-look shot.

In the instant his shotgun kicked, I leapt. Before I even knew my intention I lunged forward. His chest was thick and cold under my fists—like a slab of processed meat—and in the bitter wind it had the surface sheen of bologna. We rolled to the ground, snow crunching beneath us. I kicked the gun clear. Beckett bucked his torso under me, a spooked horse. But it was no use. I got his neck pinned under the hickory handle of the pitchfork. He made a throaty gurgling sound. My knees were on either side of his neck, forcing the handle down, down. His eyes rolled back in his head.

"Daddy!"

The sound punctured the air, a report all its own.

I looked around. Neil was running down the hill below the stable. Barefoot, wearing only jams, wind whipping the flannel.

"Go back!" I shouted. "Have Mom call the sheriff."

"Daddy, look!" He was pointing toward the llama.

"The sheriff! Have Mom call." Snow skiffed up under Neil's feet. The bare soles looked pink. When he didn't stop, I roared, "Now!"

Beckett went limp beneath me. I rolled off, eased the pitchfork's handle from his neck. His chest rose and fell in tight shallow swells. Legs twitching in the snow, he lay there, a beached thing. The bathrobe had flapped open to either side of his torso. In various places—chest, belly—his skin was mottled, the first waxy stages of frostbite setting in. I reached in his bathrobe pocket, rummaged around for more shells. Finding two, I duck-walked over to where I'd kicked the shotgun. The barrel still felt warm when I broke it under my hands. I loaded the shells, snapped it shut. The wounded llama was dragging its hindquarters, hobbling toward the herd, a slow action that had been going on ever since I'd crested the ridge. I jammed the gunstock back against the meat of my shoulder and sighted along the barrel. Stroked the trigger. It kicked, a bruising jab that winded me. The llama fell in stages—to its front fetlocks, haunches, upper chest, left shoulder. Finally, it dropped its long neck across its body, a careful and precise move, like an origami fold that even under steady hands proves tricky. At the gun's report, the rest of the herd had leapt up, as one. Now they shuffled nervously on the broken ice. I could hear it crack beneath them.

Behind me came a moan, then something crunching in the snow. Beckett was sitting up. He wrapped the bathrobe around him. The whiskey had worn off, and the shakes had set in. He yawned. Hypothermia was taking over.

"It's hell, bub. What the bitches'll drive you to."

"*You're* hell, Beckett."

"So it hasn't happened to you yet? Okay. Hang around long enough. It will."

"Beckett, the soothsayer."

He fingered the purplish bruise that was forming on his neck. "Laugh if you want. The Bitch used to go to a fortune-teller. Card reader, right? Never told her anything truer than 'You'll return somewhere you've been.'" He snorted, swiped at his nose with the back of his hand. "We always return somewhere we've been, bub. Every damn last one of us."

"Like you've returned here."

He spread his hands and tried to smile. His teeth had begun to chatter ferociously. "It's not enough, bub. A gun. To protect yourself from them. Bitches gone bad."

"It'll do."

An engine sounded from up the ridge. Too soon to be the sheriff. When I turned to look, I saw a blue golf cart zigzagging down the hill, snow flying up from its small tires, its fringe blown by the wind. Cell Phone.

Before the cart had even stopped, he was leaping out. He had on a pair of lycra running tights and a shiny Goretex parka in an apple-green shade. He took the scene in—me with the gun, Beckett sitting in the snow, the downed llama over there.

"Poacher?" he asked, eyes on me.

It hit me: they'd never met. Why should they? The way real estate got transacted out here you'd never need to. I told him it was Beckett, the llama guy. The former owner. Cell Phone gaped, stunned.

"My *God*, man!" The words kind of choked in his throat.

Beckett was pathetic, yes.

No walk-a-mile-in-my-shoes identification here. No There-but-for-the-grace-of-God-go-I feelings at all. This guy was a mess. A way you'd *never* be.

Then, lightly, like a bird landing, I felt something warm bump against my side. Neil. His small arm encircled me. At least he had on a coat and boots this time. I patted his hand.

"Dad*dy!*" he breathed, urgency in the word. He looked from our old neighbor to the dead llama, eyes focused and intense. He tightened his grip on my waist. "Dad*dy!*" He gave me a clutching shake, as if there were still more to be done.

But there was no more to be done.

The sheriff would eventually come.

The llamas would get trucked away.

In the spring, Cell Phone'd have the lower forty ripped up and a driving range installed.

Neil's First Communion would go off without a hitch.

The Angel of Death? He wouldn't ask about it again. Because we'd been there, done that.

And both wound up knowing what mercy is.

Jo-Ann Graziano

*Judging by the vinyl poinsettia tablecloth and the Advent
Calendar on the wall, it's Christmas or New Year's. That's me
in the middle holding the cheese, under the influence of the
patriarchs: my maternal grandfather wielding the Asti Spumante,
and my dad, Vinny, no doubt content from consuming all the
dried sausage except the two slices left in the foreground.*

Jo-Ann Graziano was the first woman to graduate from Harvard University's new ALM Program in Creative Writing and Literature. Her work has appeared in the *Harvard Review, ForeWord Magazine,* and the *Charles River Review* (formerly the *Brattler*). She is currently at work on a short-story-cycle novel, told in multiple character voices, of which this is the title story.

Jo-Ann Graziano

JO-ANN GRAZIANO
The Healing Power of Garlic

I am cooking out of respect for the dead. Nettie, my grandmother, taught me. Her sister Lucy, the newly deceased, was Mama Rose's other daughter. Lucy's pink formica kitchen seems freeze-dried in the 1950s, the pink countertops and white tile floors speckled in stardust, as if it had been her own private dance hall where she warmed up friends and family leftovers. I have to rummage for the utensils an every-day cook would use—a wooden spoon, a cheese grater. A plane growls overhead, the casements shudder, as I shock the head of garlic under my palm, sputtering cloves all over the counter, sacrificing some to the floor.

My mother enters with all the decorum of a 747. I crawl the floor, chasing slippery shards that jump from my fingers. I look up. She is decked for mourning, in a new black rayon tent that makes her look thinner, the way she hopes the cousins would remember her. She holds a bottle of Chianti by its neck.

"Anna, what are you doing down there?"

"Careful, don't slip, Ma."

"Get up, you'll ruin your sixty-dollar jeans." She lays the familiar bottle of wine, cradled in its straw bassinet, on the formica next to the mounds of chopped meat and waxed-paper packages of sausage.

I scoop the last clove off the linoleum, rise to my knees, and grip the counter to stand. I chuck the dirty cloves, scrub my hands, and scrounge around the kitchen.

"What are you looking for?"

"A dishtowel." I shake my hands, raining on the floor.

"Don't. We'll have to mop before they all come back here." My mother opens one drawer after another.

I untuck my black T-shirt and wipe my hands near the hem. "*Abasta*," I say. Stop.

"The limo's coming at eleven. When are you planning to change?"

"I'm not." My back to my mother, I pare the thin skin away from a single clove.

"You can't expect to go in that."

"Going." I slice the clove thinly, quick like Nettie taught me, sliding my forefinger back in rhythm with the knife.

My mother's heels clack the linoleum. She wedges herself between the fridge and the counter, addressing me to my face. This close, I can tell she's doused herself with Chanel No. 5, between her breasts, at her neck like a choker, wrung 'round her wrists. She reeks of it.

"She's your godmother, Anna."

I sweep the choppings into a bowl, lay another clove down on the cutting board, square my knife against it. "What a blessing. Like I would ever have chosen her."

"Have some respect for the dead."

I brush the remnants from my fingers into the pot on the stove. The oil sizzles between us.

The chopped meat glistens on a platter on the formica. My aunt's doorbell rings. My mother yells above the buzzer, held long as if the caller wonders if anyone's home.

"Garlic in meat sauce? Who taught you to cook?"

She knows damn well. I turn to face her. She stands regal in the door jamb. I lean against the counter, flare my chest out, grasping the paring knife like a dagger pointed toward the floor.

"My mother would never have put garlic in meat sauce. It's onions in meat, garlic in marinara. Any other way, Mama Rose would have thought was a sin."

The bell wails for attention. "Coming," my mother sings out, and departs the kitchen, summoned to her new role as family matriarch.

In the past months of my aunt's illness, my mother has phoned me, nostalgic for Manhattan Avenue. Louis Prima, Mama Rose's favorite, on the radio. Sausage seared in onions creeping down the stairwell. Her whole family living in a four-decker, in apartments stacked like ravioli boxes. Widowed when her third child Eddie was *in utero*, Mama Rose had raised her down payment frying up pepper-and-egg sandwiches at the corner luncheonette for local factory workers. Wonder woman. She chose the second floor, not too high, not too low, living with her bachelor son, Eddie, and rented the street level out to an unrelated couple the family affectionately named *Madrina* and *Padrino*, godmother and godfather.

My grandparents, Nettie and Sal, and their only daughter, Maria, had the Manhattan Avenue penthouse complete with a fire-escape rose garden cultivated by Sal. The third floor was Lucy and her husband's until Pete the butcher, the professional man in the family, made enough money to move them out of Brooklyn into their own house in Queens, directly on the flight path of LaGuardia Airport.

On Sundays, Mama Rose, always cooking, cooking, would gather some vestige of the family together for dinner in her kitchen. The meat sauce a constant, the pasta her secret— ravioli, ziti, cavatelli. Little Maria would come down two flights to grate cheese for her grandmother, followed by

Nettie and Sal, who were in time to help with table setting and wine opening. Nettie and Mama exchanged comments about morning mass being short enough. Lucy and Pete, hungover from a night of too much dancing or lolling in bed over the Sunday funnies, would descend after the rest of the family had arrived, just in time for Maria's "Blessed be God," right before the bowl was laid down on the table. And she would dress, my mother said, even for Sunday dinner. "Didn't they all, back then?" I reminded her. Not like Lucy—she almost always wore something new. Not some evening number. Macy's seal-of-approval-for-afternoon-bridge, except that our family always played poker.

My mother picks and chooses her memories—wonton soup in Chinatown with her father and aunt, 34th Street window shopping for Christmas with Lucy, and then, miraculously, Sal, dapper and unemployed as always, emerging from the bedroom with a big box, the very royal-blue pompadour coat she had fallen in love with. No mention of what Nettie, slaving her life away in a sweatshop, had given her daughter. No stories about supper with her family, late nights with her mother. Those nights Lucy was home, it seemed Maria flew downstairs to play cards or learn cosmetic secrets, returning to the fourth floor with cherry red lips that made Sal wink and Nettie send her to wash her face for bed.

For all she remembers, there are things my mother chooses to forget. And over my dead body, or at least over Nettie's, I won't let her.

The browning sausages cackle in the kitchen. I reach deep into the pot and turn them with a dinner fork, all Lucy's got. My mother toddles in, cradling bakery boxes and cellophane-wrapped cookie trays, and sets them down hard on the formica table. She brushes her hands together and sighs for effect.

"Who's here?"

My mother starts listing the litany of cousins. The grease spatters and I pull up the fork and walk quick to the sink. I run my hand under cold water.

"You burned yourself. You need some help?"

"I need a meat fork. God, did she cook at all?"

My mother finds a long-handled ladle in the tin breadbox. "Every summer, she'd treat the whole family to a night of *fra diavalo*. Lobster, mussels, scallops—delicious."

"Extravagant," I wince. My hand smarts. "In the breadbox?"

"I brought it this morning; for serving, after we get back. Didn't want it to look messy for the relatives, so I shoved it in there."

I instruct her to watch the sausages and head for the bathroom down the corridor. Another plane passes and the porcelain soap dish rumbles. My aunt doesn't have any Unguetine in the medicine cabinet, so I settle for cold cream and swaddle my hand in toilet paper.

Uncle Eddie, Lucy and Nettie's baby brother with the hermaphroditic chest, meets me in the hall. He hugs me tight, squeezes the breath out of me. In his day, he had a set like Carmen Miranda, but now his famous chest sags, flabby under his white dress shirt, turned to raisin. "How's my girl?" he pulls back, looks me over, notices my bandage. "What'd you do?"

"It's nothing." I excuse myself, explain I left my mother alone to mind the cooking. We sidestep each other, him for the bathroom, me for the kitchen, promising to catch up later.

"How's your hand?" My mother is lifting the last sausage, perfectly browned, onto a platter full.

"I'll live."

"Good. Your bandage reminds me how my mother and Lucy used to wrap their hair in toilet tissue at night, under the net to preserve their beauty-parlor 'dos.'"

"I saw Grandma do that more than a couple times."

"No *braciole*?" my mother asks. "It was your aunt's favorite."
Braciole takes a lot. You have to pound down a flank steak,
imbed pinenuts, basil, and raisins into its skin, jelly-roll and
toothpick, then fry it up. Nettie only made them on special
occasions, holidays. I don't particularly care for the taste, and
Lucy certainly wasn't worth all the trouble.

"Too much work. I got the cheese and fennel sausage
special for you."

"You want to do something for me, you could go."

"Why?" I grapple with the electric can opener, having to
hold and rotate the tomato cans for it. She starts towards me.
"How come you remember some things and others you just
seem to forget?" I breathe heavily, frustrated with the can
opener.

"You think you know everything. You don't." My mother
leaves me struggling with the tomatoes.

Sundays my grandfather would sneak into the kitchen
while Nettie was at Church and pollute the sauce with Chianti. Nettie would be furious when she got home and tasted
the sauce before adding the meat for the second half of the
simmering. "Sal, Sal, did you doctor my sauce?" He had this
way of smirking with his eyebrows, just for me, I thought, but
I bet my mother knew it too, the way they'd curl up in glee.
Then Nettie came up with the idea to preempt his tampering
by posting me on guard. She would go to church first, and
then I could go with my mother. But she should have known
Sal was a charmer. He would bribe me with a taste of wine, a
treat at eleven, then bet that Nettie wouldn't even know
when she returned.

We always ate Sunday dinner in the kitchen at Nettie's,
except on special occasions, holidays. I remember sitting at

dinner one Sunday after Sal had had a few glasses of Chianti. "Goddammit, Nettie, you're always leaving your bras hanging on the dining-room chairs. And then you come to bed wearing men's pajamas. Can't you give me anything?" Nettie just said, "Sal, why don't you go take a nap," and she began clearing the table. I offered to help but she shooed me out of the kitchen. My mother followed Sal into the living room and then proceeded out the front door, probably to take a walk. Sal laid down on the living-room couch with his Chianti bottle at his side. I went into the dining room and lifted Nettie's brassiere between my thumb and forefinger. It reeked of cooking—onions and garlic.

After God took Pete, Lucy would sometimes join us for Sunday dinner. She had taken in a boarder, twenty years her junior. She must have paid for the dancing. Sal goaded Lucy at dinner for dragging this man, young enough to be her son, out in public. I couldn't quite understand what he was talking about. Until I walked in on Lucy and Sal one afternoon *imbraciamente* in the dining room, her hand fondling one of Nettie's bra straps. I stood there, suspended in the thick scent of garlic Nettie was frying in the kitchen. Lucy caught me out of the corner of her eye, let the strap fall out of her fingers, and whispered something to Sal. They held firm together and turned their heads towards me, driving me out of the room with their eyes. I backed away, still staring full at them, and sought refuge in the kitchen.

I used to wish I had a garlic talisman to ward off Aunt Lucy. I hung a fresh braid in my own kitchen, four days ago, when my mother called with the news. Send a mass card, at least, she said. But I didn't know to whom. So I did what Nettie would have. Offered to cook. To lose myself in the sauce.

Nettie taught me. The first step to a perfect meat sauce is the garlic. You have to do more than slice it; dicing is not enough. Cut it up any way you know how, but the secret is to crush it with the palm of your knife. She never minced words, my grandma Nettie, with her dyed auburn hair. (What color it was when she was thirty like me, the black and white photos would never tell.) Then you fry it in extra virgin, and the minute they come to the door you've got them with the smell. It's the crushing that lets the essential oils out.

J. LEON 02.

Nettie always said onions made her cry. Told me that thanks to the invention of tupperware you wouldn't have to throw away the extra onions like Mama Rose did. The plastic kept the refrigerator pure. To tell you the truth, I think she peeled them when she wanted to bawl uncontrollably, wringing her eyes in the crook of her elbow. I never suspected it then. But this morning, hot oil searing, I remember the tupperware containers filled with chopped, sliced, and diced onions, waiting in the fridge for some unknown purpose already fulfilled. If only an onion could resurrect my grandmother.

You can use crushed or whole tomatoes, but she insisted you crush the whole ones into the pot by hand to get the right consistency. This takes time, but I have four generations to remember as I clench my fist around an Italian red, strangling its juice into the pot.

They descend on us like tourists, pouring out of the planes from LaGuardia, Lucy's godchildren assembling in her Flushing living room. Everyone in the family knew about Lucy's hysterectomy. And everyone knew Pete had been in the Navy. Whatever he had or hadn't given her, no one ever said. Maybe they forgave him or maybe they enjoyed his extra-thick pork chops too much. So, everyone sacrificed their first-born to Aunt Lucy. The early Christians created godparents in the time of religious persecution to safeguard their children's upbringing. Maria was born before Lucy had it out, but I doubt Nettie would have named her Maria's godmother, no matter how much Mama Rose pleaded. Lucy must have been shopping in Macy's, cool while a midwife swabbed her sister, the hot July air rising all four floors. Nettie never meant to give Lucy anything. She set Maria's hair in banana curls before work and left her to be raised by Mama Rose and Sal. Maria spent all her time with Lucy. *Madrina.* And Maria gave me to Lucy.

The tomatoes need to simmer. I make an appearance amongst my godsibs. The rich smell of browned sausages masks the scent of grief throughout the house. They linger, second and third cousins, on Lucy's crushed-velvet couches, not quite comfortable amongst her filigree bric-a-brac. I see traces of the Tucci nose, Mama Rose's thick throat, Nettie's flaky forehead, Lucy's wide eyes, though none of the men seem to have inherited Uncle Eddie's chest. Thank God. The windows rumble; someone makes a joke about the sisters bowling in heaven. Uncle Eddie will not be one-upped.

"If I were LaGuardia," he says, "I wouldn't've wanted this airport named for me."

"Why not? Every time a plane takes off, someone remembers you."

"Every time one lands—or takes off—someone curses you to hell." The room laughs, and the grief loosens.

Someone remembers Eddie's glorious return from the war and tells the story. Brazen Lucy had been a redhead back then. She had passed out pot-cover cymbals up and down Manhattan Avenue. Hell, her baby brother Eddie, skinny Ed with his jokes and his girly chest, her Eddie would be coming home. Alive. Who cared if he had only been a cook for a radio unit in South America? It could have been the end of the world. It could have been Canarsie. Lucy started the block ruckus; she would have led the tickertape parade, while Nettie helped Mama Rose prepare the *braciole*. Little Maria alternated between watching them and cymbal playing out the kitchen window.

"God, my sister was a real performer." Eddie begins swinging his hips, mimicking Lucy dressed to kill in some upstate Catskills retreat. The cousins clear a way, pull the coffee table up against their knees. The room is silent, except for Uncle Eddie swaying with all the earnestness of Vic Damone, his chest lagging behind a beat, as he belts out, *"Femina, tu si non mala, femina."* He sings all the stanzas and folds into my mother's arms as another plane descends on LaGuardia. The room hesitates, then one cousin claps, strongly, and we all follow suit.

The sauce is roiling, boiling, and I have to turn down the burner. My mother at the sink tests the water and fills a glass to refresh my uncle.

"He was beautiful," she says. She lays the glass down on the table, absent minded, and peels the foil off the wine. I stir the sauce with the wooden spoon. She knows exactly in which drawer to find the corkscrew. "I used to pour myself a glass, while she was back there resting, these last days." She uncorks the wine and approaches the stove.

"What do you think you're doing?" I say.

"Your grandpa Sal loved the taste of the wine in the sauce. Give me a little sugar, he would say."

I raise the spoon, block her way to the pot. "Grandma hated him for that."

"How can you say that? Everyone loved him."

"To hear you talk, you'd think he was either the life of the party or Jesus Almighty. And Lucy must have been the virgin Mary."

"This is her funeral. No disrespect." She crosses herself with the wine bottle. "I never said my father was a saint. Or my mother."

"Leave Nettie out of this, God rest her soul. How can you just forget?"

"I remember everything. Things you don't even know."

"I should have made a *puttanesca* sauce. Just right for the *puttana*." My mother collapses into the chrome chair as I call our aunt a Roman whore. I calm the sauce with the wooden spoon. She is sobbing.

"Where's that water? I'm not that young anymore." Uncle Eddie steps into the kitchen. He goes to my mother, kneels at her feet.

"Talk to her, Eddie, she doesn't want to go."

"Girls, girls." He says, reaching for his water. I take off from the kitchen.

Lucy's bedroom stinks of years of liquid foundation and Chanel perfumes. The walk-in closet has become a mausoleum of dresses; I wonder how my mother will get rid of all of them. Best to call the Salvation Army. In a corner, I find the button-front dusters. Even Lucy's housedresses were loud. I pick out one without too much spangle, in Mardi Gras colors. A hint of her sweat lingers in the ring around the collar.

Mama Rose. One Christmas, while she pretended to sleep in her wheelchair, I approached her with a shot glass of Sal's homemade fermented cherries. She accepted my bribe, rolled the cherries around on her tongue, and gulped them down whole. Then she grabbed both my hands. Her skin was as thin as dried sausage casing. She drew me in close, stinking like garlic. A yellowed clove hung from a string around her neck. Her husband Nunzio, she reminded me, slipped on a garlic clove and died, back in 1927. She pulled me even closer, strong for an old lady, and rasped out her secret meatball ingredient. Mama Rose believed in garlic. She had roasted garlic in that corner eatery she ran and would hang a garlic clove around Maria's neck at the first report of epidemic. My mother rarely got sick.

Nettie retired to care for Mama Rose and raise me. My mother had better sense at betting than her father. She was willing to risk more than her mother, in business, anyway. She invested her time in a jewelry line that still sells well. Before her eyes went bad, Nettie would design dresses for me. A yellow Easter Sunday A-line with daisy accents. I preferred her cooking lessons. Sitting at the kitchen table grating parmesan by hand while she unrolled the mysteries of the perfect *braciole*. Pinenuts and raisins. Nettie always said the cheese had to be grated fresh for each meal, something Mama Rose taught her. My mother would flit into the kitchen and steal a chunk of cheese that had squeezed out the side of the grater.

Lucy was always trying to coax me out from under Nettie's cooking duster. Chasing me around the house spritzing this inexpensive perfume, Charlie, in my face, saying, Little girls shouldn't always smell like garlic. Gifting me with store-bought dresses. A flouncy tutu I never wore. She kept the Chanel No. 5 to herself and she never once helped Nettie with the Sunday sauce.

After I saw them together, Lucy and Sal, I suspected I'd find a new pair of disco Candies, a silky body suit, and matching wrap skirt on my bed. I would have preferred a bottle of Chanel. Instead, Lucy stopped following me around with the cheap perfume sprayer and Sal kept his Chianti to himself.

Meatballs are funny. Everyone has her own special recipe. One egg or two. Bread crumbs or fresh bread slices. I must confess Nettie's meatballs were not the best in the family, and my mother's were always too dry. Two-day-old Wonder Bread ripped apart by hand—Mama Rose's secret. I've added my own extra, pinenuts, probably to make up for the *braciole*. Most people who taste my meatballs go back for seconds and thirds. Maria's jealous. Nettie would have been proud, although she would have thought it was unorthodox to roast the meatballs in the oven the way I do rather than frying them up after the sausages and pork.

Uncle Eddie has poured himself a glass of wine and is seated at the kitchen table, his collar up, his tie draped like a priest's stole around his shoulders. In the misty morning light, it looks phosphorescent purple more than black, a closet holdover from his disco days.

"Isn't that tie a bit loud?" I cross to the counter, unwrap my hand, and rinse off the cold cream.

"For your aunt? Are you kidding?"

I laugh, rubbing my hands.

"Lucy christened this my lucky tie. Every time I wore it, I got lucky." He crosses the tie over.

"Swear? And when would that have been, 1974?"

He pulls the knot through, too thick, and unthreads it. "Okay, you got me. Still, not half bad for an old guy." He throws his head back, sits tall, puffs out his chest. "Some girls from the old neighborhood might be there."

"You planning to get lucky?"

"Nah." He slides a perfect knot up to his neck and snaps down each crisp collar. "I'm wearing this out of respect. You think my sister would have wanted everyone moping around draped in black?"

"The way my mother sees it, I bet she would."

"You shouldn't be so hard on her," he says. "There's a lot on her shoulders."

I turn my back to him and crack an egg over the side of the bowl. It runs down into the bloody chopped meat. "Okay, so she has her reasons. Why can't she respect mine?"

"Respect?" He gulps his wine and there is a long pause. I unwrap the cheese. "Way I see it," he says, "you owe Lucy your life."

"Right." I grate parmesan over the meat, straining with each pass over the wedge.

"No. Serious."

Something in his voice makes me turn sideways, the cheese and grater still in each hand, almost in anticipation of a performance. Eddie holds out his goblet and contemplates the contents, lost in the mystery of the wine.

"Don't get me wrong," he says, "I love both my sisters."

He addresses the wine glass.

"Your grandmother didn't want your mother to go through with you. Seventeen years old, she kept saying, my baby, just a baby."

"What?" The grater bites into my raw hand.

He tells the wine, "Even made the appointment on Canal Street." He lays down the glass and turns to me. "Your aunt, God, she fought her. She said it had to be Maria's choice. Even threatened to tell Mama."

I turn back to my work, unwilling to show my face. I hear him drain his glass, smack lips, set it down. The cheese flakes over the meat like snow, but soon stains dirty with blood.

Uncle Eddie scrapes the chair across the linoleum. He walks up behind me and rubs my shoulderblade with his broad hand. "Maybe we'll see you there." He walks out of the kitchen, his jacket strewn over his shoulder, a fleeting Sinatra, to join the last carload of cousins heading for the funeral home, then on to church.

Alone in Lucy's kitchen, I plunge my hands into the cool meat, soothing my burn. I roll each handful meticulously 'round between my palms. Did she love me all those years out of guilt? The planes bowl overhead and I try to discern by the engine noise whether they're on take-off or landing. I imagine my grandmother's purgatorial kitchen, Lucy and Sal frozen together in the dining room.

When I finish the meatballs, I wash my hands. Then, I lift the lid off the sauce and lower the browned pork and sausages into the bubbling red Mediterranean. I pour myself a water glass full of wine, even though it's barely past eleven, and sit down at my aunt's pink formica table. A plane approaches, louder now than all the others, as if hurtling toward my aunt's house, on a collision course with my life.

I envision the church is dim. I would take a seat in the back, away from the family. My aunt's casket in the center of the aisle, polished to perfection just like her, seems to attract each gleam of light. The priest finishes his "ashes to ashes." It is time for the eulogy. He announces a special guest. From the back of the church a speaker approaches; the congregation turns its head, as if in anticipation of the bride on her wedding day. My grandmother waltzes out of the shadow in the flowing blue organza dress we had laid her out in, the one she sewed for herself for my confirmation. I reach out to touch her, but she strides by, intent on the altar, only stopping to pluck a rose from the spray laid over her sister's casket.

Nettie mounts the altar stairs. She takes the microphone from the priest and strolls to the middle of the altar, in front of the communion table. She looks out on her family, clasps the rose tight to her chest, and brings the microphone to her lips.

She begins to sing, "*Vo-la-re*. Vo-oh-oh-oh." The whole altar becomes her stage. The chalice and tabernacle glint candlelight. She turns and addresses the ascended Jesus, painted high above the altar, his wide arms conducting the band, then twirls back to face her audience. She strides left to right, singing, swaying hips, extending arms, just like Lucille would have in a nightclub, pulling the rose in to her breast, holding it out like a torch. At the end of the number, she blows a kiss to her sister. The family applauds. She hands the priest back the microphone and makes her exit down the aisle.

I step out from my pew. "Grandma, how could you?"

Her skin, this close, looks as dry and thin as I remember Mama Rose.

"There are things you must forgive us for. That I should have taught you." She hands me the rose. The thorns scratch my palm. And then she is gone.

Now, I hear family voices boiling over in the hall. "So many flowers!" "The priest was too long winded, but beautiful, just beautiful." I spy the opened basket of Chianti on the counter and tilt it to the lip of the pot, a big pour. Then I drain the macaroni in the sink. My mother comes in behind me. I stiffen, half-expecting her to start in on the *puttanesca* note or to bark orders about setting the food out for the guests. I shake the colander, toss the rigatoni into the big flowered bowl.

"Your hand? It's better?"

I hold it high like a priest blessing communion.

She hunches in one of Lucy's kitchen chairs, her pearls draped on the table top. She stares, as if she can see through me to the stove. She hasn't bothered to re-apply her makeup; just a hint of color remains on her lips. Her face appears worn from the memory of more than just the past four days. Then I realize. I haven't removed the duster.

"Mama Rose, Pop, Uncle Pete, Mom, Aunt Lucy," she sings at the room in a low tone. "It's over, baby, over."

The hunk of bread I dip in the pot comes up soaked in meat sauce as thick as our blood. I carry it over to her and dry her tears with the corner of the duster.

"Good," she says. "Just like I remember it." She says she sees I used the wine, and I smirk with my eyebrows, then shush her into the bathroom to fix herself for the company.

Let her stay mad at me for not going to my own god-mother's funeral. Maybe she'll forgive me when she sees me coming through the kitchen door with my pasta bowl brimming with sausage and meatballs. Family secrets are best kept in recipes.

Aaron Tillman

Mmm...pudding!

Aaron Tillman earned his MFA in Fiction Writing from Sarah Lawrence College in Bronxville, New York. He is currently a full-time instructor of English at Heald College in San Francisco. In addition to teaching, he works as a freelance writer and editor for Chelsea House Publishers. On their behalf, he has produced nearly twenty Research and Study Guides on writers ranging from William Faulkner to Flannery O'Connor.

AARON TILLMAN
The Great Salt Lake Desert

FIRST-PLACE WINNER
Short-Story Award
for New Writers

*J*an and his mother Dora moved in with Uncle Marty
soon after Quincy got mauled by the Franklin's bull. Quincy
had taken a bus up to Poughkeepsie, New York, to spend the
summer with his camp friend, Francis Franklin, and work on
the Franklin's farm, as a means of coping with the departure
of his father, Norman, who had been living with the parochial-
school teacher Helen Stripper for almost a year by then, and
had all but abandoned the synagogue and his family. Quincy
was killed a week after he arrived. It was a midnight mauling;
the Franklins were fast asleep. It was as if Quincy wanted to
die, or escape in some fantasy of King David, running through
the pasture in his cherry-red pajamas, wielding a hollow
plastic slingshot.

   For Ian it was especially hard, having been abandoned by his
father and then by his brother, and, following Quincy's funeral, his mother too lost her grip on reality, wailing away her
capacity to communicate until it was gone, buried along with

Glimmer Train Stories, Issue 43, Summer 2002
©*2002 Aaron Tillman*

her youngest son, and doused with the dirt from her own hands.

So it was Dora's brother, Marty Manzel, who decided to intervene, not quite insisting that they move from the safe haven of lower Riverdale into his Washington Heights apartment, one flight up from his grocery grill: the ethnically ambiguous Marty Mason's Grill and Grocery. Ian had just finished his final year of high school and was ripe for grocery-grill employment. It would give him time to get his head right. Reap the rewards of his labor: mental rewards, Marty explained, as a wage was something to be built over time.

Ian accepted it all. He had been understandably out of sorts since his brother's funeral and had already deferred all consideration of college. He wasn't convinced he ever wanted to go, never feeling quite comfortable amongst his peers, petty milestones, and motivations. But working had an appeal for him, blue-blooded and romanticized. It was an opportunity to get to know life and to shed the shame of suburbia where he grew up feeling sheltered from the realness of the working class, the Christian class. Were they all Christian? They all seemed Christian to Ian. And they were tougher than he was, and they would never consider Riverdale a real part of the Bronx.

So with Marty's ulterior blessings about the virtues of grocery-grill employment, Ian geared up for the gritty Washington Heights working life, eager to get his hands in a dirty bin of condiments.

But after a few weeks, this had lost its glamor. He started to long for something else, for some*where* else, away from the events of the past year. He hadn't quite come to terms with the fact that nothing would bring his brother back, nor his father, and it was just as likely his mother would never be the vibrant and religious and parentally involved person of old. So he stabilized himself with fantasies of escape. And a smattering of retribution.

Ian would gaze out of his bedroom window, into the bleak but alive Washington Heights night, and imagine himself riding over the George Washington Bridge, fleeing the wretched phonies like his father and Helen Stripper, while the world behind him fell in a storm of sulfur and fire—Ian, like Lot, escaping Sodom. It was a dream where retribution and glory came in clumps, and the instantly understood were granted solace and self-righteous providence. These were the visions that came to him at night, under the lights of the George Washington Bridge, his eyes pinned to their wounded winks of destiny.

S.LEON 02-

But Ian's idea of flight was not all fantasy, half-baked and biblical. He had a plan, a real one, directed and mapped out. He would drive across the country on the road he could almost see from his bedroom window. Interstate 80, all the way from the George Washington Bridge to the Bay Bridge in San Francisco, California. He even traced it out on his map, allowing his dream to ripen in the golden highlights of his pen. And then the fruit fell, right into his hands. Four months to the day after Cheryl jingled into his life.

Ian was standing behind the register when Cheryl walked into the store, her entrance stretching like hot dough in the yearning belly of his brain, the door chimes like dinner bells, beckoning. She strode with decadence past the cooler of salads and meats, her purple bag trailing like a berry from a bush. Then she stopped, fully formed and beautiful on the public side of the counter, and whispered: "Bathroom. I really really need to use the bathroom."

But Mr. Mason was on her like a flame, his mouth a maniacal siren blaring over the empty counter: "For Customer Use Only!"

And Cheryl, urgent as a mouse: "I'll take a sandwich."

"What kind?"

"Turkey."

"Mustard?"

"Yes."

"Bread?"

"White."

"*We don't serve...*"

"*Brown*, then."

"Pumpernickel?"

"Yes," she said and slapped a starched twenty onto the counter. *"Bathroom!"*

"Right of the cooler," Mr. Mason answered, nodding to his

nephew to make the woman her sandwich. "Pull the chain when you're through."

When she returned, Ian was panting like a pooch in heat, his emotions sweating into the folds of turkey, laid like ribbons onto the bed of her grainy, brown bread. He sliced her sandwich diagonally. He hadn't held such concern in weeks. And when he gave her the change, she smiled, her teeth twinkling like the lights of the George Washington Bridge.

"No drink?" asked Mr. Mason.

"Next time I need the bathroom."

"It's on me," Ian eeked, gnawing a crumbled bill from the fat of his front pocket.

"That's sweet," she answered with a careful slant to her head. "What do you have in cans?"

"We have everything," Mr. Mason insisted, insulted.

"I want something colorful. Nothing with caffeine."

"Grape?" Ian asked.

"Perfect."

Mr. Mason swept Ian's bill from the counter and pointed to the cooler behind Cheryl. "Thank you, sweetie," she said as she exited the store.

"Anytime," he called back.

And Cheryl took him up on it. The following day, and every day after, she was back, collecting her can from Ian.

But it was a Wednesday, four months from that day, when Cheryl showed up to tell Ian she was ready to go, to drive across country. Ian had spilled his entire story by then, all in three- to five-minute clips—the span of his break—taken always after she came into the store, sixty-five cents each time; Cheryl never leaving without her soda and Marty Mason never thinking of throwing one in on the house. But it was worth it to Ian. He had befriended a beautiful, older woman and unleashed, over an awkwardly long span, fragments of a terrible load. And by the end, he had given her all she needed to know: she would spit on his father if given the chance, and raise up his dead brother, and cast the demons out of his mother, and drive him clear across the country. She was there for him.

"My car's outside," she said. "Are you in or not?"

Outside sat a Dodge Aspen station wagon. It was green with artificial wood panels running along the sides (just another facade) and Utah plates. There was a black mesh bag filled with all of Ian's cans, emptied and colorful in the hatchback trunk. "In case we get stuck," Cheryl said. "For money. Otherwise it's art. I call it *Ian*. Starting today, a traveling exhibit."

And that was all Ian needed to hear before he raced up to gather his clothes and say goodbye to the sitting, smoking replica of his mother. "It's here!" he said to her as he roared into his room. "The dream—it's here!" he said again, kissing the matted top to her bunned-up head and fleeing with a bloated gym bag for the door. His mother remained trance-like on the couch, threads of smoke filing like ants out of her nose. When Ian bolted the top lock, he imagined it was for the last time. He prayed it was.

"I don't drive," Cheryl said as he threw his bag into the back. "I don't have a license, that is. The car is on loan. We have to return it to Salt Lake. And make a quick stop in North Platte. Nebraska."

"Nebraska?" Ian repeated. "Salt Lake? What about California?"

"It's not moving," Cheryl answered. "And this'll get us most of the way there. It's *en route!*"

So Ian, easily swayed by the likes of Cheryl, got into the driver's seat and waved at his uncle who was frowning back from the grocery-grill window. Six minutes later, Ian and Cheryl were merging onto the George Washington Bridge, the exhilaration of a thousand windmills surging through

Ian's body, both of them howling as they soared over the water.

"And if we never come back," Ian yelled, windows wide, hair whipping in the wind, "we'll never have to pay the toll!"

For the first fifty miles, Ian's mouth ran unceasingly. This was his dream now, and he wanted to bring everything he saw into the open air, to confirm that it was all really happening. When Cheryl finally spoke, she put her cold hand on Ian's shoulder and said, "Maybe it's time I told you my story."

Cheryl spoke with a gravity that Ian had not heard from her before. He realized how little he had even heard her speak as she told him of her fall from grace. She had been raised in rural New York as a member of a Jack Mormon family. Beyond the quarrels and belligerent guests that made the Molly Mormons frown, her family met ultimate disgrace when her mother was seen leaving a bar with another man. "It was bad enough being known as 'Jack Mormons,'" she repeated. "But this was double disgrace." So when she was eighteen, she fled south to the city where she lived for over twelve years, the Mormon church a fleeting memory. Until a little over a year ago, when Elder Jed came to her door and turned her life around. He told her it wasn't too late for her. That the Celestial Kingdom was not yet out of reach. But first she had to repent. She had to come before the Elders and face up to her acts of iniquity.

As Cheryl lit a cigarette, Ian asked about her acts of iniquity. What it meant. How one faced up to them.

"It's when you admit how immoral you've been," she answered. "Tell of all your wicked ways. Like smoking and drinking and stealing and all that. And by the end of this ride, I'll be done with it. All my wickedness." Then she sent a tight tunnel of smoke across the cab of the car and continued her tale about Elder Jed and how gracious he had been to give her this chance at redemption. It was Jed's car they were in. He had to fly out on a mission in the Midwest. He asked Cheryl to drive his car to him. To use the opportunity to reflect and grow. But Cheryl never mentioned that she didn't have a license. She just thought of Ian and agreed.

"But we're going to California," Ian repeated.

Cheryl slapped her open hand on the dash and said, "*How* can I gain redemption when people keep calling me a liar?" Then she softened a bit and said, "I need your help with this, Ian. Are you helping me or not?" her hand now firmly around Ian's bare thigh.

"Of course," he emitted in a startled breath.

"Good," she said, pulling another cigarette from her purple purse and lighting it with the brief glory of a match. Then she looked out the passenger-side window and started to talk about the Celestial Kingdom and judgment and resurrection. And Ian, hours away from settling in with the fact that his leg had been grabbed by a full-blown woman—Mormon or not—tried his best to offer a most attentive ear, one that would never accuse a beautiful, innocent soul of anything like iniquity.

"I'm all about salvation," she said, looking to Ian in fixed yet fleeting identification. "Do you know what I mean?" And Ian, who had lent his ear and was eager to understand, felt that now was the time to express his support, to show her his understanding, as she had done for him.

So he went on high alert for worthy words, experienced and thoughtful and worldly. And what came out was something that had been planted in his brain on countless occasions. "God's will be done," he said, and turned toward Cheryl making a slow, almost suave dip with his chin before his muscles and his accordion mind stiffened at the thought of the will which had made his father leave, and his brother die, and his mother mute, and had untangled his ties to the

Riverdale temple—not that he missed the Riverdale temple. And as a cold, wet wave washed over his forehead and face, another line of unexamined rhetoric leapt from his throat, this one from his uncle: "Life is a process of losing all perspective."

"We all lose our perspective sometimes," Cheryl said, and flicked her spent cigarette out the window. "But with guidance, we can find our way again."

Ian sat in silence the rest of the way through New Jersey while Cheryl spoke about the need to be prepared when it came time to face judgment. When they reached the Pennsylvania border, she leaned back in her seat and flipped on the radio.

"PA used to have the best radio," she said in a refreshing change of tone, her soda tone, her grocery-grill tone. "Now it's all crap."

That night they slept in Allegheny. They got a room at a motel that had two twin-size beds and a fifteen-inch television. Ian went to bed in his clothes and thought about the road, and about radio, and about whether there was such a thing as the will of God. As he fell asleep, he was anxious to drag all unresolved ideas into the more resilient depths of his subconscious.

When they started out the next morning, Ian felt more relaxed, excited, and set to fall back into the groove of the road. And though Cheryl devoted a portion of the ensuing days trying to round out his knowledge of the Mormon church, she did not push too hard. The susceptible state of his mind was clear. And Cheryl wanted to help him. Lead him down a righteous path. Align herself with Ian, and allow the radio and the road to push them closer. Then maybe Jed would take over from there. In North Platte she would show him her surprise. How pleased he would be to double his missionary merits.

So they drove through Ohio and Indiana and Illinois and

Iowa—lodging in South Bend, then again outside of Des Moines—stopping only for gas and food and Cheryl's cigarettes. They were making good time, watching the scenery roll by; they were Truckin', Ramblin', Takin' Care of Business, staring outside at the passing trees and truck stops and vast, vibrant farmlands—*America!* They hardly even had to speak.

And this was exactly as Ian had imagined it. Not that it was as clear as all this, but this was definitely it. Freedom from decisions and obligations and pressure and loss. And loneliness. Cheryl was there for him. And she had exposed a vulnerable side, too. She wanted to shed her vices and do what was right for the sake of her soul. She was all about salvation, and Ian could respect that. She wanted to return to her home town and restore her good name. Lead her family back to the light. Ian understood. And he was happy just to listen. Happy to be on the road and part of the landscape, soaking up all this experience.

But as with all good things, there eventually comes Nebraska: the open plains, the delirium of the landscape, the crosswinds like hands of hellish spirits, pushing them around the interstate. Iowa had been such a nice surprise. So green with unexpected hills. But now he could hardly hang on. And Cheryl was acting strange. Moody and elusive. Insistent that they stop in North Platte.

There was only one room left when they arrived at The Inn and Out. It was a smoking room with a queen-size bed. Cheryl said they would take it. She needed to lie down. She was unexpectedly tired.

But as they walked from the wagon to the room, Cheryl made a decision. Still haunted by the urges of earlier days, she bee-lined into the liquor store attached to the end of the motel. Ian followed behind, uncertain whether he was expected to intervene. But he didn't, and Cheryl grabbed the Maker's Mark whiskey from the shelf and bought it with two rolled-up barrels of quarters. Then they went without a word from the store to their room, where Cheryl took the plastic basin from the bathroom and walked Ian out to the ice machine.

"It's cold tonight," she said as she filled the basin. "I just can't be cold tonight."

Cheryl poured them each a drink of iced whiskey and spoke about the need to cast their evil out. With the guidance of alcohol, Ian began to feel like he understood. Things seemed okay again. Perhaps their stop here in North Platte was somehow meant to be. They might come to understand each other in a deeper way. He felt experienced, all of a sudden. As if maybe he was really here to help her.

"Have you ever kissed a woman?" Cheryl asked then, as Ian emptied the contents of his second whiskey and began to chomp the remaining shards of ice.

His face grew flush, deepening when his mind turned to his mother, Dora, the only person he had ever really kissed, aside from when he was ten and he pecked the bare arm of Agnes Berkowitz at a holiday party in the lobby of their building in Riverdale. Ian was a bud. And Cheryl knew it.

"Would you like to kiss me?" she asked then. And up to that point, he had only thought about kissing her in a dream sort of way, like traveling across the country had been: not something he ever felt coming, just something safe to dream about. But then Cheryl made his first dream come true, and now she was leading him soundly into the next. Something was bound to give.

"I could kiss your arm," he offered.

"Start with my lips," she said, pulling him onto the bed. This was meant to be Cheryl's final fling, her farewell sail on the waters of iniquity before she met with Elder Jed in the morning. Ian would be her first mate on this journey, and last in the age of immorality. And Ian was eager for experience, as she captained him out of his clothes and onto her hot, bubbly flesh. She steered him inside her and helped him balance on the wave-like movements of her body. And while Cheryl steadied him on top of her, Ian's mind split: half of him falling under her control, helpless to the whims of her womanhood, while the other half went on a journey, exiled from present events back to a life of bridges and grocery grills, funerals and deadbeat fathers. All the while Ian—if there was such a singular soul—was witness to it from the heights of the room, like a blimp of surveillance, gathering it all in, confident that Cheryl, the mother ship, would lead him back again.

But everything happened so fast. The only warning was in the rhythm of their breath, rising closer to something climactic, apocalyptic. Then the events in his brain came crashing together: every moment in a flash, as if to face simultaneous trial, biblical judgment. And in the midst of one monstrous spasm, everything stopped, suspended in purgatory, before the captain's call to order broke his freeze and his muscles began to heave, contorting like a giant marionette at the hands of a devilish puppeteer, and a flood of emotions surged through his chest, filling his lungs with quivering air. And while Cheryl shook and Ian flexed and the headboard stuttered for mercy, Ian opened his mouth, and at the top of his lungs begged, like the supplicant of an evangelical preacher, to be delivered from evil: "Oh Lord!" he cried, *"Oh Lord!"*

Ian had known that Cheryl had power, but had no idea the extent to which she could affect him. If only he could live it again. Take notes. Though he would never have that chance. Fate's cruel rule. So he searched instead for help.

He tried to talk to Cheryl. To tell her minute by minute how he was feeling. But Cheryl, who smiled at first at the energy with which Ian's mouth ran, soon began to yawn, until she finally fell asleep, leaving him to fend for answers on his own.

So he opened the side drawer and lifted out the Gideon's Bible. He had spent so many hours in the last few days hearing of Joseph Smith and the Book of Mormon—not to mention so many years, leading up to his father's departure, under the influence of the Riverdale synagogue—that he thought searching first hand inside the most pedestrian of bibles was the best way to regain his bearings. He wanted to embrace his new perspective. And what better way to start than lying naked in a North Platte motel beside a Mormon woman with whom he had just had sex, and reading Gideon's Bible?

Ian flipped through the many stories of Abraham, reflecting on the complexities and contradictions of the word of God, until his mind began to ease and his eyes began to tire, and, in that most vulnerable state before one finally falls asleep, when the brain has opened up, ready to be whisked away, he turned to the Book of Genesis, 18:1, and read through the end of chapter 19. It began with Abraham's attempt to bargain with God over the events that would make up the story of Sodom and Gomorrah. Ian read it all and then fell asleep, the book left belly down on his bare chest.

By the next morning, he found himself in a new land, one of foggy experience and naked vulnerability. The world seemed at an awkward slant, and when he tried to speak, his voice just wouldn't come out right, so he was relieved at first to find himself alone. Then side swept by the note on the bible which was closed now and resting on the bedside table. *Ian, honey, we're outside by the wagon. Whenever you're ready.*

We're outside? he thought. *We?* His face filled with the burning blood of his body, and his brain—only beginning to seam after last night's split—felt like it was stretching apart again. But through a rationality never employed before, he found a way to settle himself down and ease the blood out of his face: Cheryl had only used an expression. What was the harm in *we*? Hadn't he, after all, experienced the multiplicity of the soul only an evening ago? No one else could possibly be in this random motel in Nebraska where he had had sex for the first time and read the Bible and felt an unexplainable connection with something so close to God.

But even though he felt relieved—and he was relieved—by his ability to redirect the blood from his face to more diverse passageways—many, he hoped, leading back to his brain—he could not completely deny the anxiety that encouraged him to dress quickly, gather the contents of his gym bag, and hustle outside. And when he got outside, he made an effort to reconstruct the anxious events in the most amusing way possible, all in the what-better-way-to-show-my-new-maturity-than-to-laugh-at-my-old-self vein, which was all good and well, except for the fact that Cheryl was not alone. She was smoking a cigarette with her back turned to a middle-aged man who was pacing and pointing and flinging his arms all over the air. Ian's face burned once again, only instead of with fire, it was ice; the blood had fled, his body was pale.

"What saddens me most," he heard as he approached from the blind side, "is that you're only betraying yourself!" When Cheryl looked up and caught sight of Ian, the middle-aged man turned in a whip, his hand already extended. "Jed Vitek," he said in a tone that differed drastically from the one he had just used with Cheryl. "I understand that you're Ian."

Ian nodded, not daring to speak. Instead he stood and stared at this imposing man with his broad head and thick, wavy hair, streaked with lines of grey. There was a slight gap between his two front teeth, the narrowness matching the slim black tie that hung between the short-sleeves of his white, oxford-cloth shirt. When it was clear that Ian would do nothing more than nod, Jed opened the passenger-side door and waved Cheryl in. Then he opened the back door and asked Ian if he would be joining them for the rest of their journey. Joining them? Ian heard in some distant reserve of his brain. *Their*

journey? Exactly who was joining whom? But as horrified as
he was, he found himself stepping into the car and closing the
door, and sitting silently in the back while he was swept back
onto the interstate.

With the wheel of destiny no longer between his hands, Ian
was helpless now to the parade of sights and sounds and
incarnate ideas that rolled past and around him like attractions
in some raucous biblical carnival. The radio played softly and
Elder Jed spoke continuously, but Ian could not bring himself
to hear. Bits of earlier conversations kept creeping back into
his brain. He realized that Elder Jed was the "what," or the
whom in this case, that Cheryl had planned to stop for in
Nebraska. And Ian was the surprise that she had for him. Was
she trying to convert him? Turn him into something he was
not? It all seemed so creepy and blasphemous. He wished he
could crawl outside of his body and return to the safe haven of
Riverdale, the last place he truly felt safe, the last place where
things made sense, the last place he had a brother and a father
and a mother and a home. He longed even for the synagogue
where he used to dread spending time. He was so alone now,
like Lot after he fled from the wickedness of the world, his
wife turned into a pillar of salt after looking back at the wrath
of God.

And though Lot made it out with his two daughters, he
too had been misled. For Lot it was his very daughters who
had plied him with wine and laid with him for the purpose
of bearing children, fearing their opportunities had been
frozen away in salt. Is that what Cheryl had done to him?
Did she fear her opportunities were drying up? Was she
hoping to deliver even more Mormons to Elder Jed? Ian
needed to clear his mind. He gazed out at the cows and
cornfields of Nebraska and began to pray for Wyoming,
hoping the mountainous expanse of the neighboring state
would make things better. Perhaps the higher elevation

would bring them all a bit closer to truth.

But Wyoming was an uphill climb. And when the altitude reached seven thousand feet and the digital dial, which had once played the Ramblin', Truckin' tunes of happier days, now spun like a mad carousel through the unreceptive stations, Ian began to unravel, feeling the pressure in his nose and in his eyes and in his head. Feelings of isolation squeezed out of the drying bud of his brain, flowering, as if through shackles, from the porous cracks. He felt the need to be grounded. He was lost in the oxygenless air of Wyoming.

When they finally stopped in Rawlins for gas, Cheryl tried to say a few words to him, but he was beyond listening and unable to respond. His tongue was like birch bark, curling in the cotton air. Yet the next place he found himself was at a pay phone. He filled it with the coins that had been accumulating in his pocket for the past several days, and dialed home, longing to talk to family, feeling, with an intensity that he hadn't experienced for almost a year, the loss of his brother and mother, and even his father and Uncle Marty. He longed desperately for familiarity, perspective.

Uncle Marty answered the phone and recognized Ian's voice, despite the shrill squawk that Ian seemed to hear from his mouth.

"We have to do something about your mother and your bastard father!" he started, not asking where Ian was calling from or how things were.

"What's happened to Mom?" Ian asked, his real voice rearing out of the pasty fog. "Has something changed?"

"Nothing at all!" Marty blared back. "And if you think I'm gonna have her planted on my couch like a smoking vegetable for the rest of my life, you better think again! So I called your bastard father to tell him that he better take some responsibility for his life. And you know what he did, the no-good greedy bastard?"

Ian couldn't answer. It was enough to keep up with the rate of Marty's return.

"He shows up for five minutes and takes off. Then what do I get delivered *by messenger* to the grill today? A letter. *From an attorney!* Saying that Norman, *your bastard father*, is entitled to your mother's assets, *my family assets*, because Dora's not cognizant enough to keep them, and he's her *legal* husband."

Ian held the phone frozen against his ear. The hole which had already blown open in his brain was widened by the thrust of his uncle's words, exposing the most sensitive areas of his mind. And as a mechanism of defense, his left hand, the only part of his body that seemed to move, reached out toward the phone and hung it up, just before Marty began the next portion of his tirade. When Ian's hand returned to his side, the receiver still pressed to his ear, there was a new voice on the line, resonating and genderless, fearsome and beautiful, calming and unmistakable, exactly as Ian would imagine it to be: this, the voice of God.

And it was nothing less than God's plan that was revealed to Ian at that very moment. The world would be swept away in a storm of sulfur and fire. This world of iniquity would dry up in a desert of salt. He would be spared this evil fate in order to carry on the message of the Lord. But to whom? he wondered as he climbed again into the backseat of the wagon, understanding that he was not to reveal the Lord's plan until the formal command had been made.

So Cheryl and Elder Jed and Ian—his ear waiting for the words of God—roared out of the Rawlins service station and sped back onto the Interstate.

"Next stop, Salt Lake City," Jed said from the front, his demeanor seeming to have changed a bit. But it was too late, Ian thought.

Then Cheryl, who had all but exited Ian's world since Nebraska, decided it was time for her to speak, asking if there was anything she could do for him, at this time, in this car, on this ride that had once been exclusively with him. "I feel responsible," she said. "I was worried about your soul and I thought I could help you." She was leaning around from the front seat, staring into Ian's vacuous eyes. "My weakness got the best of me. My intentions were misguided. But Jed said he could lead me again toward the path of righteousness. Only I need your forgiveness first. I took advantage of you. Lied to you. Betrayed you. And now I'm asking for your help."

And as Cheryl looked back, Ian started to cackle, his anxiety lifting along with the maniacal ring that jabbed out of his throat, until she finally turned around, and Elder Jed made a scene out of flipping on the radio, and then another one of turning the radio down, all in an attempt to gain full attention as he decreed that Cheryl's deeds had conjured up the devil. If only they knew.

God didn't speak again until they rumbled into Salt Lake City. The snow-stained mountains looked like eyes, accusing the sky of something dreadful. And only Ian knew what it was. Jed pulled into a gas station and asked Ian to fill up the tank. When he stepped out of the car, Jed was already behind the wagon, pulling the black mesh bag out of the hatchback trunk. He was going to cash in the cans, he said. Trade Cheryl's art and Ian's investment in for fuel. Cheryl stayed in the front seat and looked straight ahead. Ian was staring at her furrowed brow when the Lord's voice came to him again.

Ian was to fill the tank and flee the station. God would spare Cheryl, too. They would ride off together, leaving the wretched, wicked world to be wiped away. Humanity would be left up to them. And Ian understood that their first child was already forming inside her.

So Ian did as he was told, topping off the tank and climbing calmly into the front seat. Then he tore out of the station, filled with such exhilaration that it wasn't until they were well on the road when he realized that Cheryl had been shrieking the whole time, demanding to know what Ian thought he was doing.

"This is a kidnapping!" she blared, in what Ian thought to be the ultimate irony. But he forgave her and pressed the pedal tighter to the floor. Cheryl's hands were clutched onto the door grips and she was pleading with him to stop. But with God on his side, there was nothing he couldn't do. He had thought that Cheryl had similar power at one point, but now he realized that it was he who was guiding her. She would understand all this soon enough. But to calm her down, he thought it best to speak, something he hadn't really done since Nebraska.

"I know that you're carrying my child," he said to Cheryl, who stopped her screaming and looked at Ian, first with shock and then with something closer to pity.

"Just because we had sex doesn't mean that I'm pregnant," she answered.

Ian returned her gaze with the assured look that only the voice of God will give someone, and he said, "Yes, but I know it's the case."

Then with equal assurance, but a bit more compassion, Cheryl said, "Ian, honey, my tubes were tied over five years ago. I can't get pregnant anymore."

Though Ian had full faith that the power of God could extend well beyond the reach of modern surgery, he felt himself tense up a bit. His foot, which had eased off the gas pedal for a brief moment, was now weighted heavily on the throttle. As the wagon screamed along the interstate, things again grew a bit blurry.

One of the last moments he remembered—and he did remember—before he began to emerge from what would eventually be termed his first psychotic episode, was Cheryl looking back over her shoulder at the blaring lights and swirling sirens of the wicked world about to meet its end, and screaming.

Ian turned away from the road to plead with her not to turn around when the wagon veered off the shoulder, rolling over an embankment and thrusting him cleanly out the front window, while crushing Cheryl inside the car's fragile frame.

Ian landed shredded but alive nearly twenty yards onto the surface of Utah's Great Salt Lake Desert. Before he lost consciousness, he lifted his head over the expanse of this beautiful, petrified stretch, the salt of sin seeping into his wounds, and he prayed, with the strength of a saint, that he was alone in this godly land, left as a token of good in a world too desperate for purpose.

SHORT-STORY AWARD FOR NEW WRITERS
1st-, 2nd-, and 3rd-Place Winners

First-place winner: AARON TILLMAN

Aaron Tillman receives $1200 for his first-place story, "The Great Salt Lake Desert," which begins on page 45, preceded by his profile on page 44.

Second-place winner: MELODIE S. EDWARDS

Melodie S. Edwards receives $500 for "Si-Si-Gwa-D." Born in Washington state in 1971 and raised in a rural mountain town in Colorado, she has published a trail guide to northern Colorado and newspaper articles on the subject. Her work has appeared in Prairie Schooner *and other magazines and her drama has been performed on stage in Durango, Colorado. She has a completed novel and currently is attending the University of Michigan MFA program in creative writing.*

"Si-Si-Gwa-D"

On Tuesdays, she goes to town. It's the only day library hours and post-office hours overlap, it's that small a town.

Third-place winner: LIANA SCALETTAR

Liana Scalettar receives $300 for "The Dead Sea." She lives in New York, where she writes and teaches adult education. She holds degrees from Columbia, Brown, and Sarah Lawrence, and has been a fellow at the MacDowell Colony. Her critical work has appeared in Queer Frontiers *and* Mujeres Fuera de Quicio. *"The Dead Sea" is part of her first collection of stories.*

"The Dead Sea"

When I'd heard from everyone but my mother, I asked her what she thought, and she said, "I think you know why you're buying all that salt." I had no idea but I kept quiet and stacked what I bought in hard-to-reach cupboards that had been empty.

We invite you to our website (www.glimmertrain.com) to see a listing of the top twenty-five winners and finalists, and our online submission procedures. We thank all entrants for sending in their work.

VALERIE MARTIN
Writer

Jnterview
by Janet Benton

Valerie Martin has published six novels to date, including A Recent Martyr *(1987) and* The Great Divorce *(1994); two books of short stories; and a work of nonfiction. Martin has remained a dedicated writer through times of difficulty and success, whether faced with the challenges of her early jobs as a waitress, a welfare case worker, and a bookstore clerk; with the duties of a tenured professor in a graduate writing program; or with the sudden abundance of*

Valerie Martin

time after her novel Mary Reilly *(1990) appeared. A retelling of Robert Louis Stevenson's* Dr. Jekyll and Mr. Hyde, *the novel*

Glimmer Train Stories, Issue 43, Summer 2002
© *2002 Janet Benton*

was translated into many languages and was made into a feature film in 1996 by director Stephen Frears.

Martin's latest book, from Knopf, is a work of nonfiction biography called Salvation: Scenes from the Life of St. Francis *(2001). Martin has taught writing at the University of New Orleans, the University of Alabama, Mount Holyoke College, the University of Massachusetts at Amherst, Loyola University, and Sarah Lawrence College.*

You were born in 1948 in Sedalia, Missouri?

Alas, yes. And my dad was a sea captain. When I was three, my family moved to New Orleans. My dad was off for long periods at sea, and my mother's family was from New Orleans. She was mostly alone with me and my sister, so it was an obvious choice for her to return.

You studied English at the University of New Orleans and spent a year in a graduate English program at Baton Rouge, then went to the University of Massachusetts, Amherst, where you earned an MFA in playwriting and published a short-story collection.

That's right. I wrote the stories in *Love* while I was in graduate school, and it was published after I graduated by Lynx House Press, which was founded by graduate students, friends of mine. They asked me to get some stories together, and they put out this little book.

What made you start writing stories instead of plays?

Well, my plays just weren't very good. I mean, when I look at them now I just die of shame. I was thinking the other day that when I look at my early stuff, I see that it was all naked and unconscious, that I had no idea what I was dealing with, what it all meant about who I am. When I look at that stuff, it seems so bare and crude, I feel embarrassed. When people talk to me about it, you know, "Why all of this masochistic stuff,"

I think, Well, I don't know. [Laughs] Looking at old work was a good experience, to be able to feel in some ways I have a lot more control now.

Do you think it's fair to say that your work has always had a strong moral and intellectual component? Your characters often struggle with those sorts of concerns.

Yeah, I sometimes get accused of that. I don't love hearing that. I want my characters to be much more than mouthpieces for my ideas, and I think for the most part they are. But in a novel, characters are under stress, and they express who they are. And if they have to face moral issues, then they have to articulate who they are in a way that they might never do otherwise. And to me that's part of the beauty of the novel— you get to put a character under stress and they get to have that confrontation, and they do it out loud.

What do you think some of the early moral influences were on you as a child?

Moral? None. [Laughs]

Was the church the first?

I was really religious as a child. I was Episcopalian, and it's very hard to be intensely religious as an Episcopalian. Although the mass is so beautiful, it's Shakespearean. It's very intoxicating. So I did have that.

Were you always interested in saints?

Pretty much, yeah. I don't know why I was so attracted to the whole idea of being a saint. I've always been attracted to people way out on the edges. I guess part of it was the idea that a saint, by being extremely good, outstrips everybody.

So it was a way of being extreme without being—

It's a way of being bad without being bad. Yeah. I like that. You know, of making people really uncomfortable, but they can't do anything about it, because you really are a saint.

In your third published novel, A Recent Martyr, *one of your characters is a novice, and she worries about offending other people with her moral intensity—and she judges them. But she doesn't give it up.*

No, she doesn't. I was trying to imagine what a saint would really be like. And Claire does have a certain kind of self-confidence. Not caring what people think—although she may know that they don't think she's very nice.

Is that a little bit about your life as a writer, that in order to write you had to be willing not to care what people thought?

Yeah, I guess so. Obviously I write because I want to change people's minds, change the way people think, make them see things they don't want to look at, and whenever you make people see things they don't want to look at, they're not grateful. So to some extent you're trying to shake up your readers, but in another sense you would like to have a lot of readers. It's a real double bind.

I'm thinking of the opening scene in your first novel, Set in Motion—*that sudden, rough sex between strangers. And Reed, the narrator's boyfriend, keeps nearly killing himself with drugs. Yet through it all, there's an emotional flatness. Was there a certain kind of complacency you were wanting to shock people out of with that book?*

No, no. When I look at *Set in Motion*, it's clear to me that the only thing I was trying to do was to find out, Can I write a novel? [Laughs] And I was relying on a first-person voice, an outsider, someone who was looking at these very self-destructive characters without judging.

You often explore the territory of extremism—keeping your eyes open, seeing the differences between kinds of extremity, not wanting to say one person is immoral or another is insane. Is there always someone in your novels who flouts convention, who's extreme in a way that makes people uncomfortable?

I think for the most part, yes, that's true. Though I've written some stories that were certainly more lighthearted.

Are those in The Consolation of Nature?

Yeah. There's one called "Death Goes to a Party" that I find very, very funny. It was experimental. But to say that *I'm* being experimental—it's like I'm asking myself, "Can I make sugar water?" when everyone else is out there synthesizing LSD. My experiments are pretty tame.

I really enjoy that tension in your work between sometimes extreme subject matter and a very controlled, very rational voice.

Yeah, I like to have that tension. It seems to me that the only way to write about extreme states is to keep your writing invisible and spare.

Do you ever find yourself writing a scene where, say, a character starts to pity him- or herself? And then have you cut that out because you don't want that tone?

No. I just don't like characters to talk about emotions unless they've got a very good reason. I think you can show who they are. Sometimes a character *has* to talk about emotions— Ellen does, in *The Great Divorce*, since she's going through a divorce.

Is it true that that novel, your seventh book, didn't get the praise that your other books did? Yet you felt it was an important advance for you.

I did, and it's not that it didn't get praised, because in fact it got really excellent reviews, and it got widely reviewed. It got reviews from people like Katherine Dunn in the *Washington Post* and Francine Prose in the *L.A. Times* and Michiko Kakutani in the *New York Times*. She had not liked *Mary Reilly*, and she liked *The Great Divorce*. It's the biggest book I've written, and with its three stories, it was the hardest book, the most complex book, and I was pretty disappointed that it did so poorly.

Did it do poorly only because you were at a whole other level of expectation? Were sales comparable to your books before Mary Reilly?

Yes. In fact, it probably did better than any of those previous books, but I guess that's how publishing is. If you have some book do well, the next one's supposed to do better, and it did not do better. In some ways I can see why; *Mary Reilly* was riding on the coattails of Stevenson. Even the Japanese bought it, not because of my name but because they knew the Jekyll and Hyde story. That gives us some idea of the popularity of Stevenson's book, that after all these years, there was no place we could find, no place in the world, where they didn't know that story. And I think another reason that *The Great Divorce* may not have done as well is that it's a pretty gloomy message. People basically don't want to hear it. Everything you can say about our situation in relation to nature is bad news. I really agree with the sentiment Katherine Dunn expressed in the *Washington Post*. She talks about the book's concern with how, in becoming civilized, we repress those survival mechanisms that in the wild we would require. So as we become more civilized, we move away from everything we had formerly been forced to do to survive. Like tearing out throats, and killing the babies that are not going to make it, which many animals still do. Animals in the wild are not civilized, as we know, yet we tend to think of them as noble. We keep trying to make animals into creatures that are somehow braver and more noble than we are. But some of them have terrible manners, and some of them are quite large. So this whole desire to save nature is the desire to preserve that which we've spent all of the last several thousand years trying to get away from. When we think of going back to nature, as somebody says in that book, we think of finding a lovely spot, and we decide, "I'll build my house here." Humans have the distinction of being the only species who loves nature and destroys it. It's a paradox. And that book also explores a theme that runs through all my books, and which I never really exhaust thinking about, which is the binary split in my consciousness—and in that, I think, of a large part of society as well—between romanticism and realism. In *The Great Divorce*, I'm pulling for realism.

At points in your career, you've killed off certain characters. I don't think there is somebody like the saintly Claire in the later books, and then by killing off Camille in The Great Divorce, *you're killing off this self-destructive, masochistic character that appeared in earlier works. Does each of those deaths reflect a change of preoccupation?*

Yeah, they definitely do. A friend of mine said, "I'm so glad you finally killed Camille." [Laughs]

Why did she have to die in that book, in that plot?

I just thought that she would. I mean, I didn't originally plan for her to die. But after the cat died, and she has those horrible experiences with men, I had a real sense that she was not going to be invigorated … I mean she thinks she could be in love with that new man, but everything flops for her. She goes in to buy sheets for him and realizes she's kidding herself, thinking they might have some kind of normal, hopeful relationship. She has that desire—but she's not one of those people who's going to get that. She doesn't know how to find a way out of the life she's in. And she is really overidentified with the cat and its rage.

Which is what happens to Elisabeth, who, according to some reviews, is modeled after a real woman who was hanged in Louisiana for killing her husband.

Not a real woman. I made that story up entirely. But, yes, Elisabeth actually does experience getting free of rage by using voodoo to transform herself into a guilt-free leopard—I mean, you can't blame animals for being vicious. You watch your cat rip the head off a bird and you think, "God, that cat!" [Laughs] You don't say, "Stop acting like a cat." Whereas if your kid did that, you would really take a different stance. Animals occupy a world in which they are not held responsible for a violent act that's part of their nature. We do not occupy the same moral space.

Not long after the movie rights sold for Mary Reilly*, you left your teaching position at the University of Massachusetts at Amherst and lived in Rome for several years. How did that influence your writing?*

After I went to Italy in '93 I didn't write very well, and I wrote very little—in the almost three years I was there, I wrote a short story and part of a novel. And it really stunned me. I was very alienated. But it gave me new subject matter. I got two books out of our time there, the St. Francis book and *Italian Fever.*

Was there something about not being surrounded by your own language that might have caused that difficulty?

Oh, it was shocking. I did pretty well with my Italian when I was studying in the U.S., and I thought when we got there I'd pick it up, but I didn't. In fact, my tongue was tied. I could understand quite a bit, but I really had to struggle to speak. At a dinner party I would have to apply every bit of energy to trying to understand what they were talking about, and then I finally got my little phrase together that I was going to try to add to the discussion, and they'd be on another subject.

So it really was silencing.

Yeah, it was. And then I started writing a book, and a different kind of voice started coming out. I wrote a hundred pages of a novel about New England. It's called *Property.* It's about a man who gets involved in a utopian community and then by a strange error, though he never ever wants to own property, he inherits lots of it. I hope to finish that book.

And then you wrote Italian Fever. *Where does that fit in?*

Italian Fever is almost a mock gothic. It's kind of like E. M. Forster and Jane Austen smushed together. Not that I can write like E. M. Forster and Jane Austen, I'm not putting myself in that company, but their influence made me want to try this particular innocents-abroad topic. It's about a young woman who goes to Italy and doesn't have a good time. Though she does have some incredible adventures and a romance, such as it is. She's quite a nice character, Lucy—Lucy Stark. It's a very carefree, rompy book. It was fun to write. I had a great time writing it. I wrote it with real ease.

What was your experience in writing the St. Francis biography?

Oh, that was torture. The torture never stops. It's like his life.

I've heard you describe how he stayed up all night praying.

Yeah, he stayed up all his life praying. Oh, you mean when he was with his friend, and his friend woke up, and St. Francis was beside the other bed, kneeling on the floor weeping and saying, "My God, my all." He did it all night long, and in the morning his friend said, "Francesco, I've made up my mind. I am going to do what you're doing, I'm going to give everything away, and you can tell me what to do from now on." That was his first brother. Yeah, that was a real research and sort of chutzpah project—it's a biography, but it's not written like a biography, it's presented in scenes. It does have some footnotes, lots of notes, about things that can be documented. Some things really can't be documented. He's a character who is too fascinating not to want to look into a lot, so I did, and I wrote this book.

What made you want to do so?

Well, I suppose in some ways he resembles my female protagonists. And people have asked me, Why are there no good males in your books? So I thought, Who's a good male? St. Francis! But it turns out that actually living out one's moral principles doesn't look so lovely.

What sorts of research did you do in Italy?

Every time I could find a place he went, I went, and I usually drove a car up the mountains he walked up barefoot, and I was still exhausted. I walked from the parking lot to the grotto or rock or the crummy little cave that he slept in. So one thing we know about him is that he had enormous calf muscles. [Laughs] He walked all the way to Egypt, so he was an amazing walker.

The book is called Salvation: Scenes from the Life of St. Francis. *Are the scenes based on the paintings you saw?*

Some are, and some of them come from old accounts, some of which may or may not have happened. For a few I was able to put him in a certain place and another person at a certain place at a certain time; whether they ever saw each other is up for grabs. This is not original to me; Peter Ackroyd does it, lots of people do it. And I've tried not to make wild guesses, and, really, I only do that once, I think. I tried as much as I could to document the scenes. Of course it was the thirteenth century, so there's a whole lot of stuff that's basically guesswork. But the story is told in succinct scenes, as if you were looking at paintings—that's the idea—which is how his life has often been told. Of course St. Francis turned out to be really pretty complex, much more complex than I'd originally thought, and his situation was so touching.

What were some of the surprises?

Well, he wasn't always terribly nice. He didn't like women. He really didn't want to have anything to do with them. The Francis–Claire story has been painted in pretty colors, but the fact is that she wanted to become a wandering beggar as he was, and when she left her family to become a Franciscan, she wound up in a regular order. I mean, they gave her a little church. Her mother came to live with her, her sister came to live with her, and they gave her a rule of strict enclosure, and she never left. So basically she was imprisoned, and she had left home thinking she was going to be as free as the little birds that Francis supposedly and probably did not preach to. So that was a surprise. But the big thing that was surprising about him was that he was against education. He didn't like the idea of people reading too much, or studying, and he was running against the grain of his time. That was when all the big universities began to be created, and he was very much angered by any brothers who wanted to go to university.

So in that sense he was a romantic, thinking that nature was where you ought to get your education?

He thought Christ's life was all the education anyone needed. Yeah. I think he probably was a real romantic. That's part of what interests me. I wanted to be realistic about a character who's totally romantic, which is how Flaubert approaches Madame Bovary. But St. Francis, besides being a romantic, is possibly the most romanticized character in the world, apart from Jesus, so to treat this basically romantic character in a realistic fashion is to demystify him and make him, hopefully, more real, more believable as a person in the daily throes of ordinary life. He lived in a violent, gruesome world and experienced years of excruciating suffering before he died—the stigmata, thirteenth-century medical treatments that included cauterizing with hot irons and bleeding. He had an eye disease that gave him horrific headaches and left him blind, and he probably had TB. For him, this was all ordinary reality. And Francesco was amazing in that he had these notions as a young man and held on to them with enormous energy and loyalty and unswerving devotion. Even in the face of the church telling him, "Stop it, stop doing this," he wouldn't. So I admire his persistence. His last years were horrible—the pain, the ill health, and his order was falling apart. His early brothers were forced to go into hiding at his death. When he died he was one of the most famous people in Italy, certainly, and even in Europe, and he was made a saint within two years of his death. And he was called a saint. He knew he was a saint before he died. When he went to a town, everybody rushed out and shouted, "*Il santo, il santo*," and tried to get a bit of his clothing, to pull his hair out of his head.

Do you think of saintly behavior as appealing?

I'm attracted to the irascibility of it. Especially somebody like him; he was determined that he would own nothing. I think that's such an amazing stance to take. His attitude was that Christ owned nothing, he was a beggar, he slept on people's lawns, and he told his followers, when you come follow me, take one robe, and don't take sandals, and don't take a bag, just walk out as you are and preach my word. And St. Francis took that as his literal guide. He never had more than one robe, which he always had to have borrowed; he refused even to own the clothes on his back. So I liked his irascibility, his refusal to have ownership of anything. It was finally forced upon him. The order broke into three parts over that question, and the winners were those who wanted to found an ordinary order that had communal property, which is what Franciscans now do have. It was quite bitter and violent. In his last years he felt betrayed by everybody. And he *was*. But it was a practical question. The church could not have twelve thousand beggars roaming around the countryside with no rules, refusing to stay in houses, going from town to town.

You went to a Catholic high school. When you first experienced Catholicism, what was your reaction?

Well, my mother had been a Catholic, and my mother's family was Catholic. And the Catholic church and the Episcopal church were really so close in their liturgy that it was no big shock to me. I had always kind of liked the whole idea of nuns and seclusion—it's very romantic and appealing to young girls—and the Carmelite nuns at my school were really wonderful. They were well educated, they were good teachers, and they were sincere in their faith—*and* they were nice. They were nice to me personally, and I have always had a soft spot for them because of that.

Before high school, were you noticed for your writing ability?

Not really. I hadn't really done much when I was a little kid. I wrote some poems and so on. But almost as soon as I got into high school, I began to be very much encouraged by my teachers, you know, with work on the newspaper and such, and I began to form the idea that writing would be what I wanted to do, so I began to practice. I knew early on that it would be a real long study, that it would take a long time to learn how to do it well, even to satisfy myself. Fairly early on I got this print of a Sasetta painting called *St. Francis's Marriage to Poverty.* I figured if you want to be a writer, you'd better marry poverty. So Francis has been over my desk almost my whole adult life. He's been my inspiration.

So in a sense, writing has felt like a vocation.

It always did. In fact, when I was leaving high school I was invited to join the convent. Only a few girls were. I guess there were three hundred girls in the school, and maybe eight would be called in to see the Mother Superior and have the talk. She was a little bitty person, about five feet tall, and really everybody was terrified of her. She was quite a little tyrant. But, you know, *good.* I liked her, Sister Mary Grace. And she asked me if I had—she said it might seem strange, since I wasn't even a Catholic, but she knew I'd certainly toyed with the idea of conversion, and she wondered if I had thought about joining the convent. I had, but I told her I had decided to write novels, and I didn't think I was going to write the kind of novels that I could write from the convent. So she told me that she did not think those two vocations were necessarily contradictory. But she didn't read any of my novels. Although, in fact, the Catholic church has been very receptive to all of the work I've done and has invited me to speak.

And you've taught at Loyola University, a Jesuit school.

And they haven't had a problem with the work. Some people have, but not the Catholic church.

So the emotions in the work really are familiar to Catholics.

Yeah. Well, Claire [in *A Recent Martyr*] is, as much as I could make her, somebody who could be considered a saint, if you understand how Catholic theology works and what it means to be a saint. I was trying to make her a legitimate candidate.

She has a couple of flaws; she's vain and she knows it. That's her little dilemma. And she's suspicious of people, and she knows it. That's a problem, she doesn't really love people; that's her Achilles heel.

It seems clear from looking at your life, at the ups and downs in your career and all the different jobs, that you've had a very big capacity for endurance and a certain intensity about your work. Is that something that you saw yourself already having as a child, or were you aware of choosing to develop that in some way?

I don't think I thought about it that much. I don't think there's any way to know how often you'll be rejected. And the way my career has been, I've always gotten—I would get a big, big pile of rejection, and then I would get a little bit of acceptance. And it would be enough to keep me going. The hardest part was after my second book [*Alexandra*] was published by Farrar Straus. I wrote my third book, which was *A Recent Martyr.* And my editor at Farrar Straus left and went to Grove. When he left he told me he would—in fact he had that novel in his hands, come to think of it—that he was going to take it with him to Grove. So I didn't think to worry. And then after he got there, he called and said there was no enthusiasm in the house, which is an expression I truly love, and so they weren't going to buy it. Then my agent sent the book out to I think twenty publishers, and it just got rejected and rejected, sometimes quite coldly, sometimes with real reservations or expressions of pleasure in the book or with someone thinking it was a good book but "not for us." And so then followed eight years in which I couldn't sell anything. I wrote three books during those eight years, and they went out one after the other to editor after editor. *The Perfect Waitress, The Earth as Seen from the Moon,* and this collection of short stories, *The Consolation of Nature,* which eventually was published. The other two were never published. I don't think they ever will be published. One of them kind of became a scrap heap; I pulled bits out of it for other things. And the other one is a very strange book. I can't figure out who wrote that book. [Laughs]

You moved back to New Orleans after graduate school, and a few years later you were raising your daughter and teaching four adjunct classes and—

And half-time at a high school. It was really hard. I don't know how I managed to do it.

When did you write?

I don't know. I did, though. I guess I wrote—I pretty much managed to get most of my classes in the morning, because I'd get my daughter to school and then teach and then go get her. I guess I did it on the weekends and sometimes in the evenings. Usually I was too tired. I don't know when I did it.

What drove you then? Did you have a strong feeling that you had something to say, or did you feel you just simply had to write?

I didn't have a strong feeling, but I just have never wanted not to write. I've had lots of friends who gave up, who said, "No, I just can't do this," who couldn't keep it going and talked with great bitterness. I never felt bitter—I never felt mad at the writing because it didn't sell. "You bad books, why won't you sell?" I felt sorry for the little books. I remember this crazy guy who wrote a short story about a writer who sends his short story all over New York. The story goes out, you know, and it comes back all fingered up and dirty, and the story says, "You shouldn'ta sent me there, how could you send me there, you're killin' me." At the end, the story's lying in the gutter, cursing him. I kind of felt like that about my writing, you know, that it was just these orphans I was producing. But I don't know, I like to write. It seems to fulfill a real need. I feel happy when I'm working on something. It gives me another world, another life, and when I was bogged down in mindless work, four sections of freshman comp. every semester, and trying to take care of my daughter, which was hard, but also very, very rewarding—but if I was writing a novel, I had this other world filled with whatever I wanted to put in it; I have another life. Something I learned over the years, and it's something I still do, whenever I'm falling asleep, whenever I'm relaxed: my thoughts turn to the book, especially at night when I fall asleep. If there's a problem I'm having, I don't mind not falling asleep. I don't mind insomnia. If I lie awake, it's a good time to think about the book, to think about a character. So I go into that frame of mind, which to me is a pleasurable place to go. It's like going to the park to go visit my book. The fact that it takes so long to write a novel, years, other people find that kind of forbidding. But to me it means I get to work in the same world and enter this imaginary place for a long period of time. I like that. The thinking about the novel is more pleasurable than the actual writing it out. I write longhand, and I write from beginning to end. The writing is dogged—that's the doggedness, which is a very good thing to have.

I once heard you say something like, "If people are questioning the details in your story, if they're saying something doesn't seem plausible, the real issue is that the voice isn't doing its job, because if the voice is strong enough, people will believe anything." I mean, look at the first line of Kafka's "Metamorphosis."

Right. "I don't *believe* he turned into a cockroach." [Laughs]

So is that what takes a while when you're working on a book in the beginning, finding the voice?

It does. Once I find the voice, then I feel quite free and happy. I mean in that hundred pages of this New England book, *Property*, I had a lot of trouble getting started. I often start too early in the action of the novel, and I wind up writing, say, forty pages before I get to the beginning, throw those away, and go on. At first I can't hear the voice, it's not coming in very clearly, it's uneven, or I don't know who this person is.

And what's the feeling when you get the voice?

You just have this sense of ease. I mean, it's a hard thing to describe. It's not mystical, but then it is kind of mystical. It's like meeting somebody. Presumably all these are voices that I somehow know. A lot of them are combinations of voices, I think. Some characters speak in the manner of people I know. Paul's diction in *The Great Divorce*, the way he speaks is very much a combination of some Kingsley Amis characters and John. So it's a voice that I'm familiar with, certain turnings of phrase, certain ways of putting things. I guess Mary Reilly's voice was the strangest to come by, because it really is so completely different from anybody I know.

Do you have that experience some people talk about, that losing track of time as you're writing?

No, generally I know what time it is. I have a clock on the desk! [Laughs] No, I'm not one of those people who writes in a blue heat, or a red heat, or whatever color. I write really slowly and painstakingly. Sometimes I listen to music. I like to listen to Phillip Glass, and I listen to the same piece every day to put me in the frame of mind. Most pieces of writing are linked with certain music. For instance, during *The Great Divorce* there were some Brahms quintets that I really liked to listen to each day as I started. I'd put in earphones and listen to them for, say, fifteen minutes and then turn it off. Then every time I heard it I'd start thinking about my characters, so I started using it to move back into the mood, the mental atmosphere.

Is there anything else you do to spur that mood?

I try to collect pictures and things appropriate to the books. I put them around the room. They're useful. I have very great difficulty reading fiction when I'm writing, and that's a real heartbreak, because I can't keep up. And there's so much I want to read. But while I'm writing, which is really most of the time, I usually end up reading a lot of nonfiction that has to do with whatever I'm writing about. I'm always writing books that need all this research. For the St. Francis book I had to read all this medieval history. I'm not a medievalist, and I still know zilch, but for a couple years, whenever I had any free time to read, I would feel the obligation to pursue that.

And you write longhand, on lined paper.

Yeah, and I keep it in a binder, and I type it up as I go along. I usually write about thirty pages and then I keep going over it and over it every day. Then I start to put it into my little word processor. The last few books have really tended to be put together in these very distinct scenes. Sometimes I have to look back; usually I don't. I worked from eight-thirty in the morning until eight at night on a recent Sunday, thinking, This is really hard. Now, I don't do *that* very often. Maybe I'm a big baby. Lots of people do that day after day. But I believe that four hours a day is sufficient torture. That thing we call work, even if you love it—sometimes it feels like mental pain. Also there is the amount of time I spend living in and thinking about my book that makes it hard for people to live with me because I'm always in another world. With John, that's okay, because he tends to always be in another world, too, so we collide over coffee sometimes, but he doesn't get resentful if I'm absorbed in a story, though I'm sure he gets tired of hearing about it, just as I might get tired of hearing about the book he's trying to finish on time. But usually we find each other's work fairly interesting.

Do you think of yourself as a child of the sixties?

Yeah, that was fun, boy. Too bad you guys missed that. That was the last time young people had a whole lot of fun and didn't have to pay. And were bad, bad, bad. Of course we did have that damned war. It was truly like a plague. Today's politics interest me because so many of our politicians are people who came to ethical maturity faced with those questions. And even people who went and fought and lost limbs are unlikely to condemn people who stood and said, Let's put a stop to this.

It doesn't appear in your work in a way that I can think of. Not just the war, but that whole time period.

No, it doesn't. I lived in New Orleans, which somebody called a hotbed of apathy.

In what sense do you think your childhood in New Orleans was advantageous for you as a future writer?

Well, it's a real spooky-story place. Everybody tells stories a lot, though I think that whole Southern storyteller thing is a myth. I think people tell stories all over. In New England, in small towns, everyone's got a weird little story. But I guess the atmosphere here is kind of gothic. And of course if the weather's warm, you can sit outside and chat all the time; stories tend to come out of that. The history of the place was interesting to me, and as a child I always was interested in learning about the people who lived here. I read the old stories about pirates in the city, and Madame John's legacy, and Madame Rilleaux, who had the slaves chained in the attic.

Did you have the opportunity to be alone a lot when you were a child?

Yes, I was alone a whole lot. And I just was mostly outdoors, walking around in the sun, getting all sweaty. In the summer I would leave home in the morning after making myself a bread and butter sandwich and stay out most of the day. I liked to be in a tree house. I had a sister, but she was three years older, and sometimes we played together, and I had a couple of other kids in the neighborhood. I don't think I was a very happy child, but I was sometimes happy when I was alone in my tree house. And I always liked animals a lot.

It seems the capacity for independence that you developed early has stood you in good stead as a writer.

Yeah, I think so. Though I don't know how independent I was as a young woman. I was quite terrified to be alone. I

84   *Glimmer Train Stories*

believed that I would go crazy. I thought I might be crazy. It wasn't until I had a child and was divorced that I realized, I'm probably the least likely person to go crazy in the world. There's nothing crazy about me.

Why do you think you were concerned about going crazy?

Oh, you know, when you're young you're dramatic, you like to dramatize.

Was there any particular thing you saw around you when you were writing your early novels that no one else seemed to be acknowledging?

Oh, I think it was just anger, rage at hypocrisy and at having to grow up a female. It's hard. When young women realize that they're going to have to be sexual objects, or, as somebody else said to me, "or not"—when you realize that you have to enter that sexual arena and what it means, it makes you angry, self-destructive, and difficult, because it's not—it's not pleasant.

Some people have been disturbed by the masochism of your women characters, especially in your earlier work. Is their masochism some kind of a protest, or do you see a similarity between masochism and saintliness? I wonder if you were pushing that in the face of your readers with A Recent Martyr *through the parallel between* Claire *the saint and* Emma *the masochist.*

Well, you can be annihilated by love or by God. I'll give you my brief summary of the real solid truth, which is that men do not cherish the notion of spiritual union, but women persist, and possibly you can have a spiritual union with a homosexual relationship but not in a heterosexual one. That's my view, maybe a jaundiced view. There's this desire to get past the ego, whether that is a rational thing to want or not. That's a part of Christian theology, Sufism, Buddhism—the notion of detachment, getting away from the body in order to get an honest view, a view that's not dying. Being in the body means you're dying. In these passionate unions, there's a way of getting around that.

It strikes me that there's something in common between your feeling about not romanticizing nature and the way you approach your characters. You seem to have an investment in being able to present them in a dispassionate way, letting them show who they are, without glossing anything over or diminishing them.

I want them to be as complex as possible, and I don't think of them as good or bad. I make a case for them. Because that's really what you do when you write a novel, you make a case for the way a person is, the way you apprehend them. I was introduced once and the guy said—he was describing the characters briefly in the introduction, and he said, "the evil Paul." And if there's anybody in *The Great Divorce* that I really think of as being like me, it's Paul. It hurt me.

You mentioned thinking about your work when you lie awake at night.

Yeah, it's kind of a discipline that I perfected when I really did have a lot of things to worry about, mostly money. And I would lie awake at night totaling up lists and figures and trying to figure out, How am I gonna get through this month? But since I was usually working on something, I found that if I would just say, Stop with the figures! and figure out what's going to happen next in the book, I would instantly become sleepy and go right to sleep.

Do dreams ever influence your writing?

Yes. Sometimes I have dreams that are solutions to problems I'm having, and they're inevitably stupid solutions. I had one not too long ago. I dreamed the solution for the end of this book that I had written six different endings for, *Italian Fever.* And I had this dream. I woke up and thought, That's it, this is wonderful, that's it. And I went back to sleep feeling happy. In the morning I woke up and examined my dream and it was just absurd. This couple goes off and starts pruning a rosebush. That's how it was going to end. It was really not satisfactory, but the dream brain thought, Oh, great solution. I get sleepy when I'm writing a lot, and a lot of times I go lie down and I think I'm going to go to sleep, but instead, before I go to sleep I start to think of what to do, and it solves the problem. I know a lot of people who do that. As soon as you lie down, all of a sudden it's clear.

Janet Benton holds an MFA in fiction writing from the University of Massachusetts at Amherst. She writes, edits, and teaches novel writing for a living. She also sings and plays bass and is cofounder of the band The Nightbirds. She is nesting in Philadelphia.

Jenny A. Burkholder

*I am the baby in the middle. My sisters, Abby (left) and Amy
(behind), taught me to trust that I could walk on my own.*

Jenny A. Burkholder has lived in Pennsylvania, England, St. Louis, Washington, D.C., Kalamazoo, and Chicago. She has a BA with Special Honors in
English from George Washington University, and an MFA from Western
Michigan University. She has worked in a record store, as a landscaper, a
reader for a blind woman, a bicycle messenger, a teacher, and an arts admin-
istrator. Her poems are forthcoming in *Spoon River Poetry Review*, and she
recently spent a month at the Vermont Studio Center.

JENNY A. BURKHOLDER
A Poem About Hesitation and Adrenaline

Ever since his headaches started, we've been more
in love. Last Saturday, we lingered in bed for hours
playing gin as the eight year old next door sang
"La Vida Loca" over and over from his bedroom.
And last night at a cookout, we stood by the grill
and hugged while other guests flipped chicken breasts
and hamburger patties. He is suddenly afraid to fly.

In my own nightmares, a 747 twists through the air
like a kite and lands on California Avenue right side up.
When I loosen the top with my electric can opener, it is only him
who has flopped over like a blow-up Nancy doll
we practiced on in CPR class while the others sip
cocktails and fill in crossword puzzle answers.

He claims his fear began at Easter when we flew over
    Three Mile Island
into Harrisburg, but these odd coincidences, Christ rising
and a nuclear meltdown can't be real. Symptoms don't know fear
and have no emotions. They do not wake up in the middle
of the night to check for snoring or feel their insides
scraping along like an old rusty muffler as they wait
for results. Dying, for some reason in my family,
is easier for the men. My grandfather was on his way

to the refrigerator for a Hershey bar and my uncle
out cross-country skiing on a crisp Vermont winter afternoon.
While the women suffer moth-eaten linens and painful
longing in the worst way. What keeps us here, wanting?

My grandmother would say it is procrastination
that secures us to the world as if dying were like
grading papers or washing the dishes. We find something
better to get in the way. She finely cuts paper with miniature
    sharp
scissors into angels and bells. But me, what about young me?
Will I have to go to sleep every night alone,
Lying awake until the glow-in-the-dark planets and stars
gummed to the ceiling slowly lose their light?

POETRY OPEN
1st-, 2nd-, and 3rd-Place Winners

First-place winner: JENNY A. BURKHOLDER
"A Poem About Hesitation and Adrenaline"
Jenny A. Burkholder receives $500 for her first-place poem, which begins on page 89, preceded by her profile on page 88.

Second-place winner: RACHEL DILWORTH
"The Magdalen Laundries"
Rachel Dilworth has recently completed a volume of poetry on Ireland's "Magdalen laundries." She has been the recipient of a Fulbright Fellowship, Yale's Frederick Clapp Fellowship, an Academy of American Poets prize, and a Breadloaf Writers' Conference Waiter Scholarship. Her poems are forthcoming or have appeared in TriQuarterly, Perihelion, *and* Ekphrasis.

Third-place winner: NICHOLAS ALLEN HARP
"Go Without Saying"
Nicholas Allen Harp attended New York University and the University of Michigan, where he received his MFA in 2001. He has won awards from the Academy of American Poets, Missouri Review, *and the University of Michigan's Hopwood Program. Harp lives in Ann Arbor and teaches writing at the University of Michigan.*

We invite you to our website (www.glimmertrain.com) to see a listing of the top twenty-five winners and finalists, and our online submission procedures. We thank all entrants for sending in their work.

Pauls Toutonghi

What can I say? I loved having my picture taken.

Pauls Toutonghi received an MFA in creative writing from Cornell University and has published fiction and poetry in the *Boston Review, Crab Creek Review, Pittsburgh Review,* and other little magazines. His story *Regeneration* won a 2001 Pushcart Prize. He is a regular contributor to juicydelicious.com, and lives, somewhat regrettably, in Syracuse, New York.

PAULS TOUTONGHI
Still Life

*P*icasso is in his studio in the Bateau-Lavoir, cooking an omelette in the wood stove. There are three brown eggs—two *centimes* each on the street this morning—and a small iron pan, black, with rust on the handle. The heat from the bulbous stove brings a slash of perspiration to his forehead. The light slants in through the windows that are high up, that are high near the top of the wall—broad windows, mouths of light, open. The omelette is almost cooked; he inhales the musk of the egg.

It is 1907, a morning in December, and this is what he is wearing: a broad, palm-wide blue tie, a white shirt with a wrinkled collar, a pair of taupe wool pants with wine stains along their length. There are nearly fifty canvases in his studio. Most of them face the walls. He has given up on painting; he sketches instead, tracing the lines of his subject with a Spanish-made charcoal pencil.

As he finishes cooking, Picasso retrieves a loaf of bread from the top of one of his smaller paintings. *My shelf,* he thinks, and opens the bag, brushes away a spider with his thick, workman's hands, rips off half the remaining loaf. Standing above the stove, he eats the omelette and thinks of the night just past, a long night, and the crooked smile of the whore with whom he's slept. He thinks of the way she half-smiled when he left, how she kissed him softly on the left side of his face.

He looks down at his eggs. *Baby chickens*, he thinks. *Infants.* He dips the bread in the yellow soup and remembers her citrine odor, the lingering scent of the sweat and stubble along the insides of her thighs. *Not unlike the smell of the eggs, actually*, he thinks, and then he is startled by a knock at the door.

Picasso pads slowly into the hallway. It is Fernande, his wife. She has opened the door and let herself in. She is walking towards him. *Damn*, he thinks. *Damn.* He sees that she is crying.

—I'm sorry, he begins. I'm sorry. I was here. All night, I was here, I swear to you.

Fernande shakes her head. She wipes her nose with the back of her wrist.

—Never mind that. You have to come quickly. Wiegels has hung himself. I couldn't cut down his body.

In the story my grandfather tells me, he is a conscript in the Turkish army.

It is 1915, and he is serving just east of Suvla Bay, a few kilometers from Anzac Cove and the fighting. It is August, and the sea kicks the linen scent of its salt into the air each day, a scent that is mixed with something else, with the sweet reek of decay and raw blood.

My grandfather's task is the assembly of customized weapons. The factory is a makeshift, dusty hangar, an enormous, single-story warehouse built from plaster and stone.

Each day, he spends his time filling forty-centimeter cartridges with high explosives, metal scraps, and a percussion cap. He then grafts the shells onto the end of two-meter-long sticks, sticks that are the thickness of a man's arm. The soldiers hurl these from one trench to the next, often during the middle of the night, when the explosion, he is told, looks like a premature sunrise.

Each morning, the colonel in charge of the munitions plant comes into the barracks and chooses a man to polish his shoes. These are luxurious, expensive, leather shoes. They have a beautiful grain; they are thin as a sheep's stomach, supple. While the soldier polishes them in the colonel's quarters, the colonel eats his breakfast and sings. One day it is a love song, one day a holy song. He has a terrible voice, and his mouth is often full of boiled eggs.

—What did you think of my singing? I wanted to be a *muezzin*, you know.

—It was very good, sir.

—It was? Would you care for an egg?

—No thank you, sir.

—Are you certain? I just bought them last night on the street. They're fresh.

When you are done polishing the shoes, my grandfather says, the colonel gives you three Egyptian cigarettes. They are cheap, sure, but the smell is unmistakable, and they have a certain prestige. You smoke them on your breaks, in front of the other men, while you perform. Sweating in the August heat, you sing the morning's songs in a steamy contralto, your voice cracking and crackling like oil cooking in a pan.

Perspective. A face, slightly deviant, arranged at such an angle. A relationship of light, a luminous body of paint, Ripolin colors, synthetic wood or canvas. Picasso and Fernande, and they are running through the narrow alleys to Wiegels's studio. It is a wet cold morning, with ice in the gaps between the cobblestones, with an occasional low-skimming gull come in off the Seine. Picasso has not slept. He has been wearing the same clothes for days, and the sweat has begun to itch, to dry and stiffen and itch. Fernande is sobbing as she runs, and he can scarcely understand her.

—We were drinking. And ether. And hashish. And then opium.

The cold air is stinging her face.

—He went home. He smiled and he bowed at the door. He actually bowed as he left. I went to see him this morning. I hoped you'd been there, you know. I hoped I'd find you on the couch.

—He did it right there? In his flat?

—Near the window.

They slow as they approach the building, and Picasso looks and sees the figure on the second floor, sees it immediately, indistinct behind the glass. He has been working, for many months, on his new method of painting the whores, on *le Bordel*, the Bordello, and now he visualizes only lines, in broken geometries and disconnected stories. The top of Wiegels's ragged boots, Picasso sees, even as he goes through the door, are still moving to the left and to the right, south and south-southwest, tracing through the air like a gentle pendulum.

In the story my grandfather tells me, he is a volunteer in the French army.

It is 1915, and he is serving near Verdun, in the low, green-stained hills. He has a new velvet hat, a freshly made *képi*, and it is causing him problems—chafing, pinching, giving him a headache.

Les barbelés, he leans forward and tells me, the barbed wire—it was like a mouth. It sucked you in, like a mouth. I was tangled once, for a moment—that's where I lost my first hat, *ou j'ai perdu mon premiere chapeau*. And such a beautiful hat, that one. A fine, nearly perfect stitching, with only one or two misplaced threads. Wool so soft you couldn't believe it came from sheep. I was glad I made it out of the wire, sure. Men never lasted in the wire—anyone could tell you that. But when I crawled back into the trench and realized that I had lost my *képi*, I wept like a little child. A hat meant a lot to you, you know, in the war.

In the war, he says and then he laughs softly, a sound dry as yeast. I was an artist, you know, a sketch painter. That didn't mean I wasn't in the fighting. I was there with all of them—with Bonnard, Moreau, Zadkine. And they were drunkards, you know, even in the trenches. I was lucky to leave the war with a liver, the way they made me drink. Zadkine especially. He was the worst. You look at his sketches—his India ink with pale blue and his simple yellow, his little cubes—and you have no idea. How could you? A tremor here, a certain translucence there? No. You just can't trace these things.

One time, I was near some fighting, near a place where the trenches had started to break down. I saw, from a distance, what I thought were some corpses in a ditch. I made my way through the field, slowly through the field, and I looked over the mouth of the hole. You were drawn to these things, you know, you couldn't help it. It was a crater from a shell, the kind that usually had bodies in it. This was no exception—two dead men, one of them missing an arm. But also—and at this I fell backwards, at this I stumbled backwards and lost my hat in the brine—there was Zadkine, sitting in the fetid water, soaked, and drinking whiskey from a bottle.

He didn't see me at first, so I waited and I watched. I was speechless, you know. He was drinking the whiskey and then he was passing the bottle to the dead men. He had pried open their mouths and was pouring the stuff down their throats. Finally, after two or three circuits, he saw my hat floating nearby. He raised his eyebrows and looked up at me and grinned; he showed me his toothy, charismatic, drunkard's grin.

—A cup! He started shouting. Why, Victor, you've brought us a cup! How nice of you. *Une tasse! Une demitasse. Une képitasse. Très bien, Victor.* Well done.

Picasso is sickened. He looks at the ground, at the walls, at the unfinished paintings that line the path to the doorway. Fernande is in the other room, in the kitchen, slumped against the wall. He cannot do what he must, and so he sits at the breakfast table near the window, a few meters away from the dangling body. There are fresh-cut flowers here— tulips, bright red and incongruous in the December day— and Picasso sees Wiegels's pipe, stuffed thick with fresh to-bacco. He waits a moment, drums his fingers on the table-top. And then he picks up the pipe, brings it to his lips. He takes the matchbox from his left pocket. He starts the flame on grout between the cold tiles of the floor.

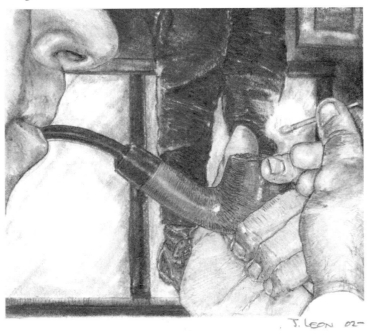

—What are you doing? Fernande has heard the rush of the igniting match, but she cannot bring herself to look around the edge of the doorway. Her voice is trembling. Have you done it yet? We need to walk to the police.

Picasso coughs a little at the unfamiliar tobacco, then exhales a mouthful of juniper-colored smoke. He looks up at the body for the first time, and notes the stains around the eyes, the terrible angle of the neck. The trail of some mucus—perhaps it is vomit—lingers along the lines of the chin.

—I'm waiting, he says to Fernande. Wiegels left his pipe. I want to smoke his pipe.

In the story my grandfather tells me, he is a novitiate in a seminary on the Italian coast, a few miles to the south of Amalfi. It is 1915.

His brothers are in the war, of course, but since he is so young—only fifteen, just like the year—he has not yet joined the fighting. The priests swish through the hallways in their laundered *soutanes*, pale and aloof, hands clasped stoically behind their backs, moving as if they are not tethered to the ground. In the mornings he prays with them; in the afternoons he pieces through the Gospels, reading, memorizing, constructing a faith and an identity; in the evenings he walks into the hills nearby and sings the mass, sings it to the sharp slip of the rust-colored land as it feeds into the Mediterranean. *Introibo ad altare Dei*, he intones, and spreads his arms as if the whole of the sea is his altar.

Then, one humid Tuesday afternoon—sometime after two o'clock but before half-of-five—he falls suddenly and passionately in love.

This is how it happens, my grandfather says, and opens his hands in the air, a gentle supplication.

I am walking to town for news of the fighting and three dozen eggs, walking along the road that I always take, wearing what I always wear, my best shirt and collar. It is rare that I am called upon to go into the village, since I speak so little of the language and am unsure of the customs. Near the last farm before the town wall, I see her: she is reading a book on the steps of her home, wearing a rose-colored hat, drinking something from a wine-colored glass. It is these colors that get me, more than anything else, these two perfectly matched colors. As I pass by her, she looks up. She sees that I am staring. She smiles at me, and notices that I wear the uniform of the would-be Jesuit.

—What are you reading? I ask.

—St. Augustine, she says. The *Confessions*.

Composition à la tête de mort, Picasso calls it, the painting of Wiegels's studio with the body near the window, done in scissored cubist forms, in minimal color.

It is late one night, only months later, and he brings it home to show to Fernande. It is a great labor, carrying this painting through the streets, this painting that is wide as his arms are wide—all heavy canvas and wire and frame. He is not a large man—this is difficult for him, a tremendous exertion. Picasso is coughing and sweating heavily when he comes sideways up the stairs. He clatters his burden onto the wooden floor of the apartment. He sees her immediately, lying on the ground, drinking red wine from a clear glass, reading a book beneath the arc of three candles.

—Fernande. Look. I brought it back. To show you. I've finished it.

She doesn't look up.

—Fernande?

—Is this the one we've been talking about?

Picasso is looking at the thing, looking at the way the paint rises from and falls back to the surface. He is looking at the places where the texture of the canvas can be seen, where the paint thins away and the fabric asserts itself. His voice is soft.

—Yes. Yes, it is. I finished it today.

Fernande stands and walks to the kitchen. She doesn't turn around.

—I don't want to see it then. Take it back.

At first he doesn't understand. He is lost in the memory of creating it, of moving his brush against the background, of choosing one shade from another, one movement from another. He is amazed at how it contains time, right there in its movements, in its angles and its subtractions. He is thinking of this and then he is beginning to understand her voice; he is turning to Fernande and he is angry.

—But it's so far. And cold. It's cold tonight, near freezing.

—I don't want to see it. Why don't you understand?

—But Fernande—

—You are so stupid, Pablo, so thick. This is my flat, too, you know. I don't want it here.

She has her back turned, and her two hands are pressed against the wooden counter. Her black hair falls like a drape, cutting off the light that would rise, luminous, from her skin. He looks at her, thinks of his weary muscles, of the weather, of the walk. Then he remembers something else. He sighs. He bends and lifts the painting from the floor.

—Save some wine for me, would you?

He leaves quietly, bumps twice into the wall as he descends the staircase.

Ted Morrissey

What can I say?
I thought I looked cool.

"Fische Stories" is from Ted Morrissey's collection, *In a Strange City*. Other stories from the collection have appeared in *Chiricú* and *Paris Transcontinental*. Morrissey, who holds an MA in English from Southern Illinois University at Carbondale, teaches public speaking and British literature at Williamsville High School, and is an adjunct faculty member at Springfield College in Illinois. He has completed two novels, *Recalling Susanna* and *Weeping with an Ancient God*. He has also published and edited the literary journal *A Summer's Reading* since 1996. He lives with his wife and three sons in Sherman, Illinois.

TED MORRISSEY
Fische Stories

*F*ische boards the train at the Fifth Street station, sheltering a hardcover book from the rain by tucking it inside his overcoat. It is forty minutes to East Abbey. He is beginning to know the route by heart: a glimpse of the grey river, buildings of steel and plastic giving way to the hulking brick two-stories, the stray-dog neighborhoods, the aging, ambivalent suburbs, then finally the wonderland of estates. Fische has no trouble finding a vacant seat. The odd midday people are far fewer than the rush-hour masses, in then out of the city. He opens the book to his marker. It is a Kawabata novel. He reads each section as if it is a poem, slowly, reflectively. From time to time he pauses to turn over the images in his mind while staring at himself in the train window, the landscape beyond occasionally intruding. He is pale, unshaven, his hair wild from the rain. He thinks he should present himself differently to Kate; but there is nothing to do about it now. Besides, this is the Fische she knows.

By the time the train reaches East Abbey he is alone. It is twelve perfectly tended blocks to Kate's house, with its brick wall and black iron gate, with its sculpted yard of old-growth trees, with its turrets and arched windows. The first view of it

Glimmer Train Stories, Issue 43, Summer 2002
©2002 Ted Morrissey

always makes him angry … sad … awed. He rings the bell and waits. Answering the door in the giant's house takes some time, he thinks. He hears her footsteps, then the silence as she looks through the peephole. She pulls back the heavy door.

"Hello, Fische." Kate is lovely and well dressed, perhaps just arrived home from a charity tea. One time he would like to find her in sweat clothes and rubber gloves, in the middle of cleaning a bathroom. Kate has people for that now.

"Hi, Kate. Can I come in for a second?"

There is resignation in her eyes as she steps back. He follows her through the foyer to a medium-size room she calls the parlor. Fische sits in the flowered loveseat and places his book on the richly lacquered coffeetable. Kate takes the ladder-back chair opposite him. He waits a moment for well-mannered Kate to offer him coffee or something, but she does not. She seems more agitated by his visit than usual.

Fische speaks toward the book. "The reason I came by—you know that box, the one you said you didn't need? Well, I didn't want to just toss the whole thing out, so I was going through it, and in the bottom were some legal pads with college notes, psych, I think, and sociology, and I remembered that you are thinking about going back to school, so I thought maybe you would want them." He dares to glance up for a moment to see her reaction.

A desperate smile takes over her face. "You came all the way out here—no, Fische, I don't care to have the old notes. Please, feel free to pitch them, or burn them, whatever you want." Kate stands and walks around behind the chair, placing her hands on its tall back. He is ashamed to see the tears welling in her eyes. "Fische, I'm sorry, you've got to stop coming out here—"

"Why, is Mikey jealous?" He is astounded at his own absurdity.

Not bothering to answer, Kate sits in the chair again. "Please listen: Michael and I are adopting a child, or at least we're trying to—it's a very complex situation."

Fische is dumbfounded.

"Our attorney tells us that during this examination period it is not unusual for the prospective couple to be watched in secret, to make sure the profile they've submitted is legitimate."

"Watched? You mean someone may be spying on you? Like a detective?"

"Yes. And Michael is afraid—I'm afraid, too—that my ex-husband coming to visit in the middle of the day, when Michael is away, might jeopardize our adoption. You can understand that, can't you?"

"This is America, Kate. People can't just go around spying on other people. It's invasion of privacy, it's uncon—"

Kate jumps up from the chair. "Fische! None of that matters. What matters is that Michael and I want to adopt this child and people may be watching us. Period." Kate goes behind her chair again. "Child or no child, you need to quit coming here, you need to move on ... for your own good. Please, Fische."

"Thank you for the advice. However, I'm not having any trouble with moving on. For your information, things are going great at the college. There's every indication I'll get a full-time position next term. There's a publisher who's interested in my book. And on top of that, I've been seeing someone, and it's getting serious."

"That's fantastic." It is clear that Kate doesn't believe any of it.

He gets up from the loveseat. "I have to get back. I apologize for showing some concern and risking your adoption. I hope everything works out for you." He turns to leave the parlor.

"Fische."

"Yes."

"Your book."

He pushes the book-laden cart through the narrow aisle, glancing at the titles. He is in world history. Fische spots a title, *Commodore Perry Opens Japan*, and takes the thick volume from the shelf. The cover is noisy with age and the pages emit a pleasingly musty scent. He begins to read and in a few minutes he is slumped in a sitting position on the cold tile floor. Scenes of Far Eastern opulence bloom like a wild garden in his imagination. He is so entranced by the words, he doesn't hear the footfalls on the tiles. Suddenly, it seems, young Miranda Harper is standing there above him. Materialized. At eye level with her knees, Fische notes the adolescent thinness of her legs.

"Mr. Fische, Mrs. Hamilton has been waiting for you to come back." Miranda's voice holds no reproach, only simple fact. "We have a loan request she wants you to locate. I'm at the desk." She holds the slip of paper.

He gets to his feet, leaving his finger in the book as a marker. Miranda smiles. "I'm sorry, Mr. Fische. I can get the book while I'm up here."

In the six weeks of knowing her, he has not seen Miranda smile. He thinks there is a prettiness behind the patchy red acne and overlarge glasses. "No, no ... I'll pull it. Go ahead back to the desk." He watches as she skitters away. He tries to sense her shape in the wool skirt and cotton blouse; but the fabric is too loose. Fische thinks back to their conversation. He hopes he didn't sound agitated.

He deftly finds the requested book and carries it downstairs to the information desk, where Miranda is sharpening little pencils for the periodic-guide table and card catalog. "Here you go: *Flight of the Enola Gay*."

Miranda stops grinding the pencil and takes the offered

book. "Thank you, Mr. Fische." There is respect, nearly admiration, in her voice. He heard it upstairs also.

Fische leans against the counter. "Where's the boss?"

"Her office. Requisitions, I think."

He thinks for a moment. "How's school going?"

"Fine. Love some of my classes, hate some. You know."

Fische nods. "Which ones do you love?"

"My modern-foods class, and creative writing. I could write and write all day."

"Really?" He thinks of Miranda writing and writing, the yellow pencil dancing ardently across the page, the tip of her pink tongue showing in the corner of her mouth. "That's great."

A man comes to the information desk. He holds out several slips of paper with scribbled call numbers, like an offering.

Fische says, "I'll let you get back to work."

For the rest of the evening, as Fische reshelves books, his mind leaps from image to image: Kate holding her blanket-wrapped baby, Miranda feverishly writing, Matthew Perry marching into a lustrous Japanese palace, all gold and silk. As if dreaming, the scenes meld together. Kate becomes both the explorer and the bejeweled empress; Miranda—grown up, porcelain skinned—holds the new baby. The incongruous mental pictures make him uneasy.

At closing time Fische and Miranda exit through the library's back door, which locks behind them. Their boss, as usual, is staying late. In the time that Miranda has been employed there, they have come to this point a dozen times. He has turned one direction toward his efficiency apartment on the edge of the college campus and Miranda has gone the other way to the closest bus stop.

On impulse Fische says, "If you're interested in writing, you should go to the Paris Street Coffeehouse. A lot of writers and artists call the place home."

"I've heard of it. I've been wanting to go."

"I'd be happy to take you there sometime, introduce you to some people."

"That would be great. Thanks."

He pretends to see his watch on the dark street. "I don't know when you have to be home, but I have time now—if you feel like it."

Miranda, pretty in the feeble light of a distant streetlamp, appears to weigh the invitation. "Sure. I have some time."

"Are you sure? Maybe you should phone."

"No, it's all right. Sometimes I stop at a friend's house."

They begin their walk to the coffeehouse, twelve blocks away. He feels a pang of shame, being out with this teenage girl. Yet he has done nothing wrong—merely invited a young writer to a coffeehouse where he might introduce her to some established artists. Yes, it is all right. Fische notes that the earlier rain has given the night air an autumn-like crispness.

"What types of things do you like to write?" he says.

Miranda puts her hands in the pockets of a nylon windbreaker, which is out of place with her skirt and blouse. "I was writing a lot of stories. Now, though, we're studying poetry, and I love that, too."

Fische nods.

"Is that bad, do you think? Should you focus on one type of writing, just fiction or just poetry?" There is notable anxiousness in her question.

"No, I think diverse writing experience is good—especially at your stage." He feels it is an appropriate time for Miranda to inquire about his writing. Surely she knows.

"That's what my creative-writing teacher at school says. He's really interesting—not like most of my teachers. You should talk with him some time."

The idea of his conferring with a high-school teacher, as if equals, irritates Fische. "Uh-huh."

108   *Glimmer Train Stories*

The city streets are strangely empty. Fische feels good about the desolation. He doesn't want to be seen with the school-girl, at least not by strangers. The coffeehouse is different. There he can introduce her to people he knows, carefully clarifying their connection. He thinks about the scandal at the college during the spring semester: the instructor and the female undergraduate. The college officially discouraged rela-tionships between faculty and students. He glances at Miranda's profile. This is different. She is not a student at the college. They do not have a relationship. He is simply intro-ducing her to local writers and artists, encouraging her inter-ests.

Fische, beginning to feel chilled, is glad to reach their destination. "Here we are." It seems that the city is unpopu-lated because everyone is in the Paris Street Coffeehouse. The noise of conversation and scent of smoke reaches out to them even before they open the door.

Fische looks around inside for someone he knows well. He only sees the faces of more remote acquaintances. Miranda points to the far corner where a table for two is unoccupied, incredibly. He leads the way through the narrow aisles be-tween overcrowded tables. Many customers are standing. They are especially congregated near the long wooden counter, to Fische's and Miranda's left as they wade to their small table. He nods to faces he recognizes. Some return the gesture. They take the unclaimed seats.

Fische leans forward. "As crowded as it is, I don't see too many people I know."

Miranda's thin eyebrow flares once to demonstrate her comprehension. The near-smile she has had since entering the coffeehouse is unwavering.

It seems they have arrived between sets of an acoustic folk band. The trio, with their six- and twelve-string guitars, step into the tiny stage area in the back of the coffeehouse, and the leader—a black-haired woman of Asian descent—speaks into the microphone. "The opening set was our 'family' portion; now we're going to perform some material that is more 'adult.' I hope no one is offended."

There is laughter from the crowd. Fische looks across the table at Miranda, who has twisted around to see the performers. Great, he thinks. Miranda turns back toward him and her expression is unchanged. Placid, contented.

They listen to a song, then another. Some of the lyrics have obscenities but nothing that a teenager hasn't heard a hundred times, Fische assures himself. At the end of the second song he leans across the table. "Would you like something to drink?" He is hoping to find someone he knows.

Miranda answers over the applause. "A latté would be great. I have some money."

"That's all right." Fische is standing.

"Thanks."

The coffeehouse is even more crowded than when they arrived. It takes him several minutes to reach the counter and order two lattés. Meanwhile he scans for familiar faces; but now he recognizes no one in the dark, smoky room. He carefully returns to the table with the hot ceramic mugs. He tries not to act surprised when he finds that Miranda has lit a cigarette. The half-empty pack is on the table.

"Here you go," he says.

Miranda blows smoke up and toward the wall. "Thank you."

He sits and is about to explain how he hasn't found anyone to introduce her to when a hand touches his shoulder. "Mr. Fische!"

It is Brenda Schnelling, the chair of the English department at the college.

"Hello—" he says, not knowing what to call her.

"How do you like the music?" Brenda Schnelling is heavy boned, blond, about fifty. Normally she wears dark suits; it is strange to see her in blue jeans and a college sweatshirt.

"It's great." He recalls hearing that she has become divorced. Involuntarily he looks at the glowing white band on her finger where the ring had been. He wonders if his own mark is so visible.

Brenda Schnelling says, "I was looking for some friends but it's hard to find anyone in this crowd."

Fische hesitates. "You're welcome to join us until your friends show."

"Well... if you don't mind. I *am* tired of orbiting." She turns and speaks to the group behind her who has an extra chair. Then, using the hand that isn't holding the coffee mug, she straightens the chair around. Fische half stands and tries to appear to help.

When Brenda Schnelling is seated, Fische introduces her to Miranda. "We both work part-time at the public library," he explains, "and Miranda is an aspiring writer." He hopes that Miranda looks older, smoking and drinking coffee; then, instantly recalling the scandal at the college, he hopes she doesn't look older.

Brenda Schnelling and Miranda shake hands. "What do you write?" asks the older woman.

"Stories and poems. Right now mostly poems."

Fische thinks, Please don't mention your high-school class... He listens anxiously to the conversation for several minutes and realizes that a camaraderie has developed between the two. Was it because of their being female? he wonders. Brenda Schnelling is literally old enough to be Miranda's mother. Yet here they are chatting like old friends— classmates at a reunion—after only ten minutes of knowing each other.

Brenda Schnelling is giving Miranda her office number and

telling her to bring her writing by some time—"Really!"—when one of her missing friends comes up from behind.

"Here you are, Bea. We were about to give you up!" The friend, a woman whom Fische does not recognize from the college, awkwardly hugs Brenda Schnelling around the shoulders. "We have a table over there." She motions nebulously over the crowd. "We've been saving you a place."

Brenda Schnelling smiles as she stands with her empty mug. "Thank you, Mr. Fische, Miranda, for taking care of me." As she pushes her chair into the table she adds to Miranda, "Do that."

"I will. Thanks."

Brenda Schnelling and her friend are absorbed into the crowd.

Fische drinks his latté, in spite of a slightly bitter taste. Miranda appears to be quite pleased, moving her head with the rhythm of the folk band, smoking cigarette after cigarette: a part of the adult coffeehouse scene. They don't bother to talk over the music. Fische holds onto a small piece of satisfaction. He has done what he promised. Miranda is introduced.

When the band finishes its set—with a song about abortion from the point of view of the fetus—Fische says, "Even though it's the weekend I have an early day tomorrow. Shall we go?"

Miranda blows smoke and puts out her cigarette. "All right."

They leave the coffeehouse and walk up Paris Street toward the nearest bus stop. A colder breeze has stirred and Fische hopes it is cleansing him of the coffeehouse smell. Buildings stand on either side like the dark walls of a canyon.

"Thank you, Mr. Fische. That was fun." Miranda seems the teenage girl again.

They come to the bus stop, where an older couple waits

beneath the shingled canopy. There is no one else around.

"Here we are," says Fische. The older couple does not acknowledge them. The bus has not arrived.

"Mr. Fische, don't you live near here?"

"Yes—a few blocks that way." He waves toward the east, toward the college's campus.

"It's still early yet. You want to get some wine or something and go back to your place? I have some money."

Fische is startled. "No ... not tonight ... no, I don't think that'd be a good idea." He wishes for the rumbling squeak of the bus.

Miranda looks down at the poorly lighted sidewalk. "I'm sorry." She has regressed beyond adolescence now; she shows the hurt of a little girl.

"Don't be sorry. I appreciate the thought." It is true, but it doesn't brighten her mood.

Miranda looks up, avoiding Fische's eyes, and pretends to search the canyon-wall buildings for something important. Soon the bus arrives and he watches Miranda walk through its lighted interior until she chooses a seat—on the opposite side. Then Fische walks away from the idling bus, through a cloud of diesel fumes as transparent and persistent as a dream.

In his sleep Fische believes he hears the high winds of a storm, but realizes, awake, that it is only the train running past. And he realizes there will be no more sleep this night. He uses the bathroom and comes back to his cramped bedroom to dress: the same pants he wore to the coffeehouse but a clean T-shirt and sweater. He thinks of Miranda's invitation. Was she high on a dose of maturity and merely wanted to extend the rush a while longer? Or was it some awkward attempt at seduction?

He looks at his rumpled single bed and tries to imagine

Miranda there. The picture won't materialize. Instead he sees Kate, younger but not prettier. It is not imagination, however; it is memory.

Fische walks through his dark apartment, deftly missing the stacks and stacks of books and papers and magazines. He finds his overcoat on the back of the couch. It still smells badly, but it's the only heavy coat he owns. He feels the inside pocket to

make sure the notepad and pen are still there. There is an all-night cafe on Fifth Street—college people and cops.

On his way out the door he thinks of the box of Kate's things and he considers taking it outside to throw away. But after a moment he does nothing with it.

The night is indeed cold. He turns up his coat collar and puts his hands in his pockets. He likes the feeling, after months of heat and humidity. He takes a detour through the campus and follows a lighted path between the college library and the west-side dormitories. Fische notices the peeling paint on the war-built, married-student housing. Then he cuts back onto Third Street and heads in the direction of the cafe. On the river a barge blows its mournful horn.

A rare car passes on the street. And Fische feels the city's loneliness, like a friend's.

He sees something move on the sidewalk several yards ahead; a cat, he guesses. But then it passes briefly through a band of yellow light and Fische sees it is too big for a cat. And it does not move like a stray dog. It seems to vanish in the shadow of a hedge. He comes to the spot and is surprised by the small child standing there. The child releases a fearful sob and hurries on ahead of Fische. In better light he sees that the child, three or four, is a black-haired little girl wearing only a pair of underwear. She half runs on stubby, unsure legs.

"Wait... stop!"

She turns around to look at him and runs faster. Fische hears her release another sob. He follows her but keeps his distance. He looks for a lighted window—for someone who must be searching desperately for this lost little girl. There is no one.

"Wait... stop... where's your house?"

She runs faster.

He thinks he must pick her up. But that would surely scare her—and what if someone comes by then and assumes the worst? A divorced man out in the middle of the night chasing down a virtually naked little girl. He remembers his lunatic reflection in the bathroom mirror.

Without even looking she crosses a street that is quite busy in the daytime.

"Hold on... please... stop! It's all right." A car passes behind Fische and he tries to wave it down, but the driver appears to pay no attention.

He closes the gap between the girl and him. She is beyond crying now. She moans, almost an animal sound, in desperation, in terror. She stops for an instant and looks around wildly, at Fische, at the high buildings, back at Fische, then runs on. He is within thirty feet—not running but walking unnaturally fast. The little girl has taken him away from the cafe and they are in a section of the city he doesn't know well at night. They are going toward the riverfront. I have to do something, Fische thinks. A block ahead another car passes and again he tries to stop it, flapping his arms, shouting. The car doesn't even slow. A barge horn sounds again on the river, which is only a blackness between the corridor of buildings; the horn is close.

The little girl slows to a walk. Fische trails her, ten feet. She continues to emit the desperate moans but they are weaker, almost below perception.

They have come to a small plaza with concrete benches surrounding a fountain with arcs of water colored by lights. Perhaps it was the sound of the water that attracted the little girl. She crawls onto a bench, which has to feel like a block of ice, and instantly falls asleep. Fische approaches her cautiously, as if she is a hibernating animal. Her sleep breathing is regular. She lies in a fetal position, shivering. Her bare skin is dark against the cement bench. Fische removes his coat and wraps it around her. She is so small—smaller than he realized—that he can double the coat over her. Even this does not seem like enough. He removes his sweater and pillows it under her head. He feels the silkiness of her hair on his fingers.

Now what? he wonders. Surely someone will come along and help him with his burden. It is only a matter of time. He looks at his watch: two, two and a half hours until daybreak. The night sky is clear. He recognizes Ursa Major and Minor dipping in the lavender blackness. Fische rubs the cold out of his arms and looks at the sleeping little girl. Then he sits on an adjacent bench to begin his patient vigil.

Dawn Karima Pettigrew

I try to pray as often as I breathe.

Dawn Karima Pettigrew is the author of the novel *The Way We Make Sense*, published this year by Aunt Lute Books. She is a two-time finalist in the North American Native First Book Award Competition, recipient of an Honorable Mention in the National LookingGlass Poetry Competition, and first runner-up in the Wick Poetry Contest Student Division. A graduate of Harvard University, she holds an MFA in Creative Writing from Ohio State University. She has served as a minister and missionary.

Dawn Karima Pettigrew

DAWN KARIMA PETTIGREW
The Marriage of Saints

*I*f I am a saint, I was born one. The third daughter of a third daughter, I broke the continuity of girls named Sao in just one way. I was wanted.

My parents, Juan Henry and Sao, like every other set of parents in our part of Kentucky, had good sense enough to know they wanted a boy. Boys are easier to raise, everybody says, and it certainly costs less. For our family, living on commodity cans of potted meat and what could be peaches or pears, boys made better sense than girls. Instead of spending the seasonal income that my daddy made drilling wells on ruffled dresses and patent-leather Mary Janes, they could buy socks and T-shirts and hope for the best. Boys could be turned out into the future to make their way, but girls required watching until they were safely folded into taffeta and lace and given away in plain view of the Messiah, all the saints, and every great-aunt that could count backwards from nine.

So it was a son they were wanting when Mami bent double over her sewing machine. Clutching her belly, clawing at nothing, she delivered a daughter, eight months along and perfect. Only one thing marred the beauty of her delicate eyelashes and her tiny fingernails, complete with opal half-moons at their base. She never breathed. Mami and Papi called her Sao and buried her in the family plot over at Our Hope of Perpetual Help Church. The whole thing hurt, but they were young and there was plenty of time, or so everyone said.

Eighteen months later, my mother went into labor. They were weeding the garden, trying to grow potatoes. My mother struck the earth with a hoe three times and bent over. Sao Number Two slid into the world one hundred and eighty-six seconds after the hoe fell to the ground. According to my father, who told it to his mother, Rhoda, Sao the Second breathed exactly twice and sighed. "She never did open her eyes," Daddy told Abuelita.

"Too good for this world," was always how Abuelita finished the story.

It was just about all my parents could take. On his way from burying my second sister, Papi stopped in the vestibule of the Our Lady of Perpetual Help Church, and stood amidst the gallery of wax saints that stared beatifically into a glory that none of us could see.

Papi balled up his fists and cried out, "If any of you are listening, tell God to give me a child!" Well, I was born in County General exactly nine months later. Papi never could tell which of the saints it was that was listening, or even if it was God Himself, but he always gave credit to St. Dominic, on account of he was standing right in front of his statue when he hollered out like that.

Back to the saint situation, being the third girl of a third girl gave it sort of a mystical quality. Add to all that, being born on All Saints' Day just about convinced Mami and Abuelita that all the saints had helped in my conception, which meant that I must be as much saint as sinner, to say the least.

Saintliness and madness appear to be close cousins. About three weeks into the third grade, the class pet—a hamster named Sid—died after Rob Adams dropped him on the ground. The other girls screamed and the boys looked out for blood, but I scooped Sid up in my palm.

"Oh God," I asked, "please make Sid live again."

Remarkably, the rodent started breathing, his little hamster lungs puffing out small sighs. The other children clapped. I was just as surprised as anybody in the room. My teachers sent a note home. I played well with others, they said, but my religious zeal raised red flags of caution. By the time of my thirteenth birthday, I was well known in Egypt, Kentucky, for dreaming things that came to pass. Miss Kennewick, the high-school counselor, suggested to Mami that I might have been a little left-of-stable.

Mami disagreed, called it persecution on account of my saintly tendencies. She carried me over to the Independent Baptist Church, but they warned her that all this trouble comes from worshiping idols and praying to Jesus' Mother. Mami repented and drove around in circles until she found herself way out in Perryville, right in front of a big tent. Like a circus tent, only nothing is funny that goes on underneath. A lean, spare man in a night-colored suit stood in the front, shouting about the close proximity of hellfire. Hundreds of people moaned, lifting their hands and shouting right along with him.

For Mami, sainthood is a simple thing. It is a condition, like being born with flat feet or favoring your left hand. Attending Flaming Fire Pentecostal Christian Church on the Rock does not endanger my saintly status in the least. In fact, when I become a missionary, it will only help.

Saul of Tarsus fell off his horse and Matthew left his job. God calls me while I fold laundry. Sleeve to sleeve, once over, I fold Papi's cotton T-shirts. He is not particular about much except laundry. White means white, he says. Mami figures that my nearness to sainthood means that my robe in heaven will be the whitest of all of ours, so she delegates the washing to me. I am on my third shirt when I hear, big as day, "Indians." Well, I hear it in the kind of voice that makes you not even care if the laundry wrinkles. I fall on the ground and begin to weep, great big tears that would make a crocodile jealous. Only I mean every one.

"Oh God," I sob, wiping my eyes on one of Papi's prized T-shirts, "I don't want to go to India. I don't want to go so far away from Mami and Papi and Abuelita and Mammaw. But I will, Lord Jesus, I'll go anywhere you want me to go."

It is right then that God talks to me. Right out loud. Like the sound of water all running together at the same time. "Who said anything about India? I said Indians." Now you can believe that if you want to, it doesn't change my life if you don't. This is my story, and I'm telling you how it happened.

Mami and Papi are so proud they about bust. They clap their hands together, shouting that now I am a shoo-in for heaven. They hug each other and run around talking about how their girl is worth three boys. "Let's go on over to the church and celebrate," Papi says. They grab jackets and go out the door, headed over to the third night of revival at the Flaming Fire Pentecostal Christian Church on the Rock. Papi suggests that they stop by Our Hope of Perpetual Help Church and thank all the saints on the way over to the service. Mami, who replaced the saints with Foxe's *Book of Martyrs* a while back, says that all the thanks should go to God. They go out of the door, and I hear their Buick start up and head out our gravel driveway.

I am alone with God. That's about how it is for the next five years, serving on the Creek Reservation in Alabama. I am alone with God. I mean, I see people, I teach Vacation Bible School, and I visit the sick and afflicted. I lay the palms of my hands on them and they get better. People bow their heads when they walk by. Voices carry, talking about how my prayers can change the weather. This is on account of the drought we had back home in Kentucky a couple of years back. I went outside, laid on the ground, and asked God to make it rain. Preachers from the Methodist Holiness Temple and the nuns from Sacred Heart of Jesus Convent did the same thing, I should add. Whether it was coincidence that it didn't start raining until I got up off the ground, I don't know. Anyway, that kind of carried the saint thing over this way.

That is, until I meet Bo Notices. That's his name. Like mine is Sao. The first time I meet him, he comes into the back of the Amazing Grace Pentecostal Holiness Church. The cinder-block church was built six months after I was born, by a teenage preacher that had seen it in a vision. Only has six members, so a general evangelist comes over from Sylacauga once a month and preaches about working while it is day or abiding in Christ or the soon return of the Lord. It's always one of those three sermons. The other Sundays, I lead singing and hold a Sunday-school class and then I testify. That's what they call it when women talk in church.

So it's after that when Bo Notices wanders into the cool dark of the just-ended service. Everybody has had a hand-shake and sung "When We All Get to Heaven" and filed out the back door when he comes in. He surprises me and I drop all five copies of the Broadman Hymnal.

"I'm sorry," he smiles. "Bo Notices." He bends over and picks up the hymnals. The back of his wrist brushes my ankle. My breath catches in my throat.

"Notices what?" I ask.

He grins. His teeth are perfectly square, lined like blocks in his head. "Notices. That's my name. My daddy's name. My grandaddy's name. But not my great-grandaddy's name."

He hands the hymn books back to me. I take them and put them on the second pew from the front, where Sally Rideout usually sits. A ladybeetle is walking across that pew. Good thing Sally Rideout isn't here. She doesn't share her seat with anybody, man or beast.

"Why not your great-grandaddy's name?"

Bo Notices grins again. "His name got changed on the

census. It was originally Notices-Rain, on account of my great-great-great grandaddy could tell you to the minute when rain was on the way."

So can I, I think, but I keep that to myself. "Oh. So what can I do for you, Brother Notices." Notices-Rain, I want to say, but I remind myself that after the census, it just isn't that way anymore.

Bo Notices tilts his head and looks me in the eye, which makes me shy. "I want to meet God."

"God?"

"God. Folks around here seem to think that you know Him pretty well. So I figured if I met you, you could at least tell me where to find Him."

"God?"

Bo Notices chuckles, low in his throat. "God."

"Well, it isn't like He's got a street address. You find God in the Bible..."

"I've heard all that," Bo Notices stops me. "I've even read the Bible—stole a Gideon one from a hotel in Texarkana. But I want to find God."

I'm calculating the possibility of finding God in a stolen Bible, when Bo Notices says something to me that nobody has ever said and probably never will say yet.

"There's something of God in the way you smile."

"What?" I can't recall ever seeing Bo Notices before, much less smiling at him.

He grins again. "I watch you. I've been watching you. You smile at people and they smile back like the Queen of England just complimented them on their dress. That's what made me think you might know where to find God."

"Well, I've got these tracts on The Four Steps to salvation..."

"No! No thank you. Not one more road map or manual or set of directions. I came to find out how to find God."

All of a sudden, I am not so sure that sainthood equips you for the job of evangelism. Bo Notices laces his fingers together, and begins to sing, "Here is the church, here is the steeple, open the door and see all the people. I know I can come to church or go practice yoga or something. But I don't want to do something and hope God shows up. I want to meet Him personally."

"I understand." And I do, too.

He sighs. "So what do you do?"

I shrug. I am glad that I wore my white sailor dress instead of the grey cotton dress that dips in the front. "I guess I just talk to Him. I just greet Him and talk to Him and He talks back. Just like a regular conversation. So far, He's always replied. He's never been rude yet."

Bo Notices's brows come together. Then he smiles, light all over his face. "Okay. Okay. Talk to Him and He talks back. Talk to Him and He talks back." He sticks out his hand, shakes mine. "Talk to Him and He talks back." Bo Notices repeats this as he strides out the church door.

I sit on the edge of Sally Rideout's pew. Talk to God and He talks back. I wish all of life was this easy.

I eat my wish seven days later. Bo Notices is sitting in the third pew on the left-hand side as the song service starts. He sings off-key, but heartily, along with "When the Roll is Called Up Yonder" and "What a Friend We Have in Jesus"— first, second, and last verses. He listens to my testimony about I Chronicles 4:10, nods as I tell about a man named Jabez, whose own mother named him after the Hebrew word for pain, but in spite of the bad start, he asked God for blessings and got a good finish. Then we take up the offering and Bo Notices puts in fifty dollars—our biggest bill yet. After that, Sister Mabel Carter testifies for the Lord. So does Brother George Lyons. I don't expect anything else to happen, so I start to close the service.

Bo Notices stands up. "Excuse me, preacher," he says. My face feels hot.

"I'm not a preacher," I tell him. "I'm a missionary."

"Missionary, preacher, whatever," he answers. "As far as I'm concerned, you're a saint."

The word hits me somewhere I can't name. I've heard it all my life, but coming from Bo Notices, it's different.

"Ladies and Gentlemen of the church, I met God."

Everybody gasps. Evidently, they know something about Bo Notices that he hasn't let me in on yet. Bo Notices grins at them, showing all of those wonderfully square teeth of his.

"Yes, I met God. Thanks to this preach—missionary here, I went riding on my motorcycle. I stopped by the river and I said, 'Hello, God. If you are there, I'd like to introduce myself. My name is Alphaeus Notices, but everybody calls me Bo.'"

I interrupt before I can help myself. "Alphaeus?"

"Yeah," Bo Notices replies.

I feel like I'm watching my life, rather than living it. "Where'd you get Bo?"

"*Dukes of Hazzard.*" I nod. Bo Notices plunges forward into his testimony. "Anyway, I introduce myself to God. 'I think that it's about past time that we met,' I tell Him. 'I hope that we can talk and maybe get to be friends. I have done a lot of bad things and I'm sure that You've seen them or heard tell of them, but I'd like to mend my ways and be a better person. So if You'd like to talk to me, feel free at any time.'"

Sally Rideout looks at him, bug-eyed. "So then what happened?"

"Nothing."

Everybody looks like you just let the air out of them. I can see their minds turning back to chicken and cornbread and beans waiting on the stove. Bo Notices claps his hands together.

"At least not at first. I sat there and sat there and finally, I figured that either God's not up there or He doesn't have anything much to say to me. So I get up and as I throw my leg over my Harley, I hear, 'A pleasure meeting you.' Just like I'd hear you. So I sit back down and talk to God and He talks back." Bo Notices gestures to me. "Just like you said He would."

Sister Carter turns toward me. "You told him God would talk to him?"

"Well, I ... Yes, Ma'am. Why not?"

"Why him? He never says anything to me," Sally Rideout whines.

"I didn't mean to make it seem like God plays favorites," I venture, trying to make peace, "I think He'd probably talk to anybody."

"Obviously," says Jenna Rideout, Sally Rideout's former daughter-in-law. She used to be married to Sally Rideout's second son, Geronimo. It's a long story. And, no, his given name isn't Geronimo. That's one thing about this part of the country, nobody is who they say they are.

"Well," Bo Notices says slowly, "I appreciate y'all's patience and I just wanted you to know that I am a changed man. God talked to me and I aim to be His friend." He sits down. I rescue the service with "We're Marching to Zion." I am glad when we all go home.

Home. That's one place where sainthood is truly important. I live in a trailer in back of the Amazing Grace Pentecostal Holiness Church. Pictures of flowers and sayings from the Psalms cover the walls. I am lonely, but that seems to be a prerequisite for sainthood. Church ladies bring me cobbler, dumplings, and chicken on Sundays, but they never invite me to eat with them. I figure it's one of them knocking on the door, three Sundays later.

I open the screen. Bo Notices waves at me.

"Hey," he says, "wanna go riding?"

He has a Harley parked in front of my trailer—well, the church's trailer, really, they just let me use it. Now, I have never ridden on a motorcycle in my life. There's another thing I haven't done, and that's wear pants. Saints in slacks are frowned upon.

"I can't." I start to close the screen.

Bo Notices catches the door. "You won't get mangled, I promise."

"No, that's not it. It's just that I can't wear a dress on that thing." And that saints on motorcycles jeopardize their saintly status.

"I figured that." Bo Notices hands me a bag from Walmart. I pull out what looks to be a skirt, only it isn't. "A skort," he explains. "Like pants only you can pull the front part over and it looks like a skirt."

Oh. I take the bag.

"Take your time," Bo Notices tells me, "I'll be waiting. Take all the time you need."

I turn around and enter the trailer. I try to hurry, only I can't. When I come out, I apologize for taking so long. I had to find some tights to go under the skort.

"It's all right. I told you to take your time. I told you I'd wait."

Bo Notices smiles at me. I know he means every word.

The sun is setting when we return to the trailer. Going to bed early is another rule of sainthood. Work while it is day, rise and pray while it is yet night. I climb off the Harley, keeping my eyes on the ground.

"Thank you," I tell Bo Notices. "For all of it."

"You're welcome. You told me how to meet God. I figured the least I could do is take you riding."

Bo Notices rides away. I watch him until he becomes very small.

I cannot tell you how the rest happens. All I know is that

Bo Notices and I go fishing and cook our fish in foil over the campfire. We go walking on trails that lead through dogwood and ferns. I do not know how I end up eating flan and hominy with Bo Notices. All I know is that I am placing dishes in the sink when I feel him behind me.

"Sao," he says. I have never heard him use my name before. "You are a beautiful woman."

I drop the silverware. Forks, knives, spoons, clatter against chrome.

"Missionary." The word slips out before I consider how much it will weigh.

"Woman. You were a woman before you were a missionary. And as a man, I'm asking you to marry me."

I forget to remember to breathe. Bo Notices kisses the back of my neck. Slow and sweet, like he's leaving something there instead of taking it away. My knees give and I feel his arms around me, holding me up. "This is what I'm going to do," he says into the back of my neck. "I'm going to leave you be. All I ask is that you ask God if you should marry me."

All my thoughts are in broken, odd angles. "Fair enough."

"One thing extra," he whispers. I nod. It's about all I can do to do that. "Do whatever He says."

"Saints do not get married," Mami says over the phone. "They are either already married, or they stay unmarried. They do not get married." She pulls out *The Saints' Companion* and slams it on her kitchen table. It sounds loud, even all these miles away.

"You are ruining all our plans," Papi adds, talking on the extension.

Things do not get any better outside my kitchen. I run into Sally Rideout at the market.

"I just think," she sneers, "that a minister of the Gospel, such as yourself, should not be taking up with such a person as Bo Notices." She lowers her voice into a whisper that can probably be heard in Canada. "He's done *time*."

"We've all been convicted, Sister Rideout," I tell her. Her eyes widen. "Of sin, of doing wrong, that is. We just got saved so we don't have to pay for our sins."

Things get worse. The postman, the grocer, the funeral director, and every church lady who spots me takes the time to tell me the same things. Bo Notices drank. Bo Notices got a Caddo girl pregnant and she had an *operation*. Bo Notices was arrested for DUI. By the time they get through, I expect to hear that Bo Notices was born with horns and a tail.

Bo Notices and I are making supper in my trailer. I told Bo Notices how the Primitive Baptists used to drop the Bible on the floor and preach whatever it opened to. He suggests that we make supper the same way. We drop the Pentecostal Ladies' Circle cookbook (a fundraiser from 1942) on the floor and it opens to "Decoration Day Dinner"—ham and pineapple, green beans and egg salad. I don't eat pork, and Bo Notices doesn't like eggs, so we drop it again. This time, we fare better, with "South of the Border Supper"—tacos, refried beans, and green onions. We skip the onions, boil ears of corn instead. Bo Notices begins to sing "La Cucaracha" at the top of his lungs. Way out like we are in the middle of nowhere, no one can really hear us.

Except for the denominational elders at the front door. They clear their throats loudly as they knock. It's their trailer, they could have just come in, but they knocked. Bo Notices stops singing. I smooth the sides of my chignon as I open the door.

"Hello, Sister Sao." The first Elder and the second Elder speak in unison, in the type of voice that is usually used for funeral homes. Jack Sprat could eat no fat, I think, since the first Elder is spare and the second is stout. His wife could eat no lean. These men were young once, I think, and then I know they never were.

"Brethren." I open the screen and they come into the front room, where the kitchen blends into the space where Bo Notices stands.

First Elder straightens his tie. "Sister Sao, we are concerned..."

"Very concerned." Second Elder chimes in.

"With Christian concern..."

"The concern of the church..."

"About the company that you seem to be keeping..."

"With such a one do not eat..."

I sink into a kitchen chair as the door closes behind them. Hell, fire, fear, and God. Suddenly, I am very tired. Bo Notices puts his hand on my shoulder.

"Sao?"

"Yes. I'm sorry, Bo."

Bo Notices sits in the chair next to mine. It doesn't match, but is higher above the table than my chair, which has one short leg.

"Don't be sorry. They're right, Sao. I was a rough customer. I drank, I fought, but I never did time. And that girl? She's got my child, married a Choctaw guy. I can't do anything about my life then, but I trust God to work in it now."

"God forgives," I start. Blood presses noisily against my head.

"I ain't worried about God," Bo Notices says. "I know He forgives. It's people that don't."

He reaches his hand across the table.

"Listen, Sao, this is what I want to know. Just this one thing. Do you think, even for one second, that they might be right? That you might lose your salvation and go to hell over me?" His eyes are large, pleading.

Who was it—Penelope, Hermione, the saint that refused to marry? Perpetua? My whisper comes out raw and verges on a sob.

"I don't know."

Bo Notices nods. "Well, I won't cost you heaven."

Once he rides away, the quiet is painful.

Alone is a state where you need an imagination. Mine wanders, focuses on Bede and Bernard of Clairvaux, makes stories of St. Thomas, who spent a sultan's money building castles in heaven, and Blessed Kateri. I wish myself on the back of that Harley. Then I repent. I read all of the prophets. The Book of Nahum makes me cry.

Somewhere left of three in the morning, I hear a pounding on my trailer. Insistent. I stumble out of the bedroom as the front door opens. That's one thing about saints, to practice sufficient hospitality, you can't ever lock your doors.

"Sister Sao, come quick," Jenna Rideout pants. She looks peaked. Despite Pentecostal prohibitions, she must usually wear foundation makeup. "Geronimo's been in a bad accident. We need you to come lay hands on him so he'll live." Without her cosmetics, Jenna has freckles. She looks young and scared.

She drives me over to Baptist General. Pentecostals don't have hospitals on account of believing in divine healing and all. So in spite of our doctrinal differences, we're grateful for the Baptists.

"Geronimo was driving. Drunk. He hit a tree. Bo Notices was passing by, and went for an ambulance."

Bo Notices. The name pinches my heart. Hard.

When we pull up at the ER, we run in. Pretty much the entire congregation and quite a few Freewill Baptists—from Geronimo's daddy's side—await me.

"Oh, Sister Sao," Sally Rideout cries out, "go in there and heal my baby."

I step behind drawn curtains. Tubes and wires thread their way in and out of Geronimo Rideout's body. He gasps for air.

"Geronimo," I say, tasting the urgency. "There's no time to

waste. I know you believe in Jesus, did when you were a little boy." Geronimo Rideout tries to nod. "Now, Geronimo…" His breath wheezes and I realize that he is trying to tell me something. I bend my head to hear his whisper. "Nathan, I mean to say, Nathan, you need to trust God right now. I mean, nobody can help you as much as He can. Will you trust Him?"

Nathan squeezes my hand.

"All right then, just ask Jesus to save you."

Nathan Geronimo Rideout breathes out three words, "Jesus, save me," before the monitor flatlines. Doctors and technicians fly to the bedside. They push me aside. The Rideout family passes me, shoving their way close to the curtained cubicle. I need to get some air.

"I heard what you did." The coal-colored face of the orderly behind me shines like the sky in Kentucky at night. "I think you're a saint."

The words sink in for a moment. "No," I tell him. "Not a saint. Not anymore. I don't think I ever was."

I walk through the electric doors of the emergency room. Bo Notices is waiting for me. He holds out his hand. I take it. No matter how they tell it, wax and plaster have nothing on flesh and blood.

Siobhan Dowd of International PEN's Writers-in-Prison Committee in London writes this column regularly, alerting readers to the plight of writers around the world who deserve our awareness and our writing action.

Silenced Voices: Anna Politkovskaya
by Siobhan Dowd

Anna Politkovskaya

*T*he *Daily Telegraph* reports that "she looks more like a spinster aunt than a hardened war correspondent" and the *Guardian* suggests she is Russia's "lost moral conscience." To human-rights professionals she is a heroine in her time; and to her teenage children, her recent exile renders her an all-too-absent mother. But all agree that Anna Politkovskaya is a devastatingly honest journalist, with the highest principles of fairness. She sees many sides of a problem, but never flinches from reporting what she witnesses.

But she is also a virtual lone voice crying in the wilderness. While the world reels from World Trade bombers and the "war against terrorism" in Afghanistan, the goings-on in the small enclave of Chechnya are on the global back burner. President Vladimir Putin has visited President Bush's ranch in Texas and has had tea with the queen, but no world leader has yet dared to suggest that his military's treatment of Chechen civilians smacks of a Milosovic-style ethnic cleansing. A spate of bombings in Moscow by Chechen separatists has on the contrary given him carte blanche to deal with his local "terrorist threat" in whatever style he chooses. Anna Politkovskaya is one of the few Muscovite intellectuals to raise a protest.

A special correspondent for the respected bi-weekly *Novaya Gazeta*, Politkovskaya received the 2000 Golden Pen Award from the Russian Union of Journalists. Grey haired, bespectacled, and robust, she led a busy life as mother and war reporter at the pinnacle of her career, until last October, when a series of sinister death threats caused her to flee to Vienna. The threats arose in response to her series of startling and deeply troubling stories about Chechnya, which she has frequently visited. A compilation of these dispatches—dating from 1999 and 2000—has appeared in English under the title *A Dirty War: A Russian Reporter in Chechnya*, published by Harvill Press. Although it has won wide acclaim, she nevertheless reports feeling horribly silenced. As she put it in a recent interview, "What torments me more than anything is the thought that those people who wanted to stop my work have succeeded."

Chechnya, a corner in the northern Caucasus, has been conflict-mired since 1994. An ethnic and religious mix (Russian/Chechnyan and Christian/Muslim), its calls for autonomy led to a preliminary war in the mid-1990s, from which the Russians withdrew after suffering heavy casualties. However, warlords took over and the region devolved into a bandit-style state. One of the parties conducted a series of Moscow apartment bombings, in which some two hundred died. This led to Putin's government declaring war again, this time with greater vehemence. The military has now been fighting for over two years. Grozny, the main city, is, Politkovskaya writes, "a living hell. It is another world, some dreadful Hades you reach through the Looking Glass. There are no signs of civilization among the ruins—apart from the people themselves." Amidst the exploding shells and gunfire, she reports, children live as if unconcerned. Mass graves have been unearthed. Russian soldiers shoot innocent civilians for no discernible reason. If you don't give soldiers at the military checkpoints a "Form 10" (code for a ten-rouble bribe), you risk a bullet in the back. "Any discussion of human rights is silly," says Politkovskaya. "Such rights simply do not exist." Two thousand civilians have disappeared, with no redress from the courts. There is no accountability for the federal troops' excesses. Reports of torture in custody are routine. She concludes: "The overall picture of the Chechen ghetto is not just grim, it is incomprehensible... What does Putin want in Chechnya? What, in view of the fact that not one of the goals of the anti-terrorist operation has been realized? The terrorist leaders are still at large. And the resistance easily replenishes its ranks with new recruits seeking revenge of the suffering and deaths of family members."

In February 2001, Politkovskaya was briefly arrested while in Chechnya's mountainous south. Russian soldiers allegedly threatened her with rape and execution while she was investigating allegations of torture inflicted on Chechens in custody. She was formally accused of infringing on the strict laws that control media coverage of the conflict, and ordered out of the enclave. In the autumn, a colleague of hers with good military connections warned of increasing danger should she pay another visit. She considered his words; but her promise to bring money for a severely burned boy's much-needed operation impelled her to return.

On her arrival she found the atmosphere in Grozny more tense than before. However, the head of a new investigative federal commission spoke with her, acknowledging some of the problems that had been occurring with the military. An hour after this encouraging conversation, the helicopter in which he and his commission were travelling exploded. She reported the incident, casting doubt on the official claim that a Chechen fighter on the street had shot it down, since, as she observed, the heavy military presence that day was such that no fighter could have moved without being spotted.

On her return to Moscow, her editor telephoned her and warned her to stay home. The Ministry of Defense apparently knew the contents of her article before it had even been published, and had told him that while her conclusions about the incident were germane, the story should not come out. He also told her that a military man called Lapin was reported to have issued threats against her. The editor suggested he provide her with a bodyguard, and she agreed, but further, more-insistent threats came, saying that her guard would not save her. At last her editor urged her to leave; she reluctantly but hurriedly did so, and has remained outside the country ever since.

She is planning a second book, which will analyze the overall effect of the Chechen conflict on Russian society. She notes a resurfacing of such phrases as "enemy of the people," a rise in racism and intolerance, and a "tougher, less polite" atmosphere. Where, she wonders, will Russia's growth of a "great-power mentality" and "warrior" ideology lead? But more than anything else, she worries about her children, who continue to receive anonymous threatening calls at their Moscow home, and hopes to be reunited with them soon.

Letters requesting that the threats against Anna Politkovskaya be thoroughly investigated, and that journalists be allowed to report on Chechnyan issues freely, can be sent to:

His Excellency Vladimir Vladimirovich Putin
President
The Federation of Russia
The Kremlin
Moscow, Russia
Fax: 011 70 95 206 5173

Laurence de Looze

*In our house we learned to read music before words.
This picture was taken just before a family recital, when
I was five. One brother played piano, one played violin,
and I played cello. Nowadays we all play the piano.*

Laurence de Looze has published fiction, essays, and translations in the *Anti-
och Review*, the *Ontario Review*, *Carolina Quarterly*, *Northwest Review*, *Exile*,
MSS, and other journals. A native of Oregon, he now lives and teaches in
Canada.

LAURENCE DE LOOZE
Correspondence

(for Maria del C.)

Esto no son cuentos.
—F. Ayala

*I*n the pedestrians-only streets of downtown Groningen, the Dutch provincial capital thirty kilometers from the
North Sea, there is a little café called *Om de hoek*. Most
afternoons a middle-aged man named Alberto, an Argentinian by birth, stops in. He orders water for tea, then pulls out a
pack of cigarettes and a bag of a green herbal substance called
maté. He usually sits by the window at a round table from
which you can see the old city and the canals.

Customers occasionally stare when Alberto draws a small
gourd with a metal straw out of his coat; he places some of his
herb in the bottom, pours the hot water in, stirs the mixture
slowly, and then begins to suck the liquid through the straw.

A few moments later a woman enters and takes her place
across from Alberto. For perhaps a quarter of an hour the two
sit in silence, sipping the liquid and passing the gourd back
and forth between them. Both smoke, even though Alberto is
a doctor.

Alberto's practice is mainly old people. In recent years he
has begun to grey himself. He has also begun to grow around
the waist—what he sees as the normal settling of a man's
chest.

He came to the Netherlands as a refugee and has been in the country long enough now that he no longer complains that things close up early at night or that good wine and plentiful sunshine (they come down to the same thing) are rarities. When asked publicly about his situation, he expresses his profound thanks to the Dutch government. In private he admits that he still finds the inhabitants of his adopted country crushingly boring.

All in all, Alberto hardly looks like a man who was once arrested, imprisoned, and tortured as a terrorist.

When Alberto first arrived people used to ask him to speak on political events in his country or sign human-rights petitions. Whenever there was a change of government back in Buenos Aires, he would be called by local reporters for commentary on the situation. When Alberto returned to Argentina in 1984 to testify on "disappeared" people during the *Junta*, the Amsterdam alternative press ran a small profile. A television crew from Britain made a documentary about Alberto. As far as Alberto is concerned, they presented his case as a political fairy tale in which everything turned out happily in the end. When Alberto saw the completed film, he smiled that smile which is not really a smile and shook his head.

The film crew didn't quite get it right. In part this was because you have to be South American to understand the full labyrinthine horror of those years. But it was also because he had held back some information.

The British documentary is entitled *The Correspondence*, and it tells the story of Alberto's experience as a political prisoner. Since it was made with Alberto's consent, the filmmakers had access to family photos and personal documents. There are slow zooms into the black-and-white image of Alberto as a schoolboy, shots of his parents, and even a fraction of footage taken during a student demonstration in 1973 in which, amazingly enough, Alberto is quite recognizable (the British filmmakers claimed not to know whether the footage came from the government or from news archives). Someone managed to single him out in the sweep of the camera across a line of parading demonstrators.

Alberto was a medical student at the time.

The documentary begins with how Alberto was arrested, detained, and dumped in a secret detention center. It then presents the story of the letters Alberto wrote that all began "*Querida Rosario,*" some sixty-five in all, of which only seven have survived. The film narrates how Alberto met Carmen and how they fell in love.

The film (which lasts about thirty-five minutes) has been shown on several college campuses in the U.S., to human-rights groups, and even in one film festival, where it was quite well received. The film crew was given access to the warehouse, converted into a men's prison, where Alberto was held, as well as to the adjacent machine shop that served as the women's prison. The story of the letters is movingly told, and it is not uncommon for viewers to have tears in their eyes afterwards. After all, a tale of two prisoners, complete strangers, who manage to write back and forth each week, who get to know one another and gradually fall in love, has all the right elements for pathos: innocence, innocence crushed, irrepressible human spirit. "It has an element of hope," one of the filmmakers told Alberto at the time, "like Anne Frank."

"It has only contradictions and paradoxes," Alberto thought. "Though not all of them."

The film starts off a little slow. The first seven minutes tell of how Alberto, fresh out of medical school, was sequestered and

imprisoned for having treated a *guerrillero*. This was about a
year after the *Junta* came to power. Alberto was working in a
clinic at the base of the Andes. During an interview in the
film Alberto explains: "Many poor people were *guerrilleros*,
and many *guerrilleros* were poor. I didn't distinguish between
them"—that sly smile again—"and neither did the military.
Treating the poor was subversive by definition."

The great irony of Alberto's capture—which is well treated
in the documentary—was that the *militares* failed to capture
him when they first went for him. They only got Alberto
because he turned himself in.

Alberto was sleeping on the top floor of his parents' house
after a forty-eight-hour shift at the clinic, when soldiers
started banging on the door. His mother, who had just returned from the market, didn't even know Alberto was upstairs. Ironically, the noise of the soldiers woke Alberto, and he
hid under the bed until they left. (To this day Alberto does
not know why they failed to check under his bed. God
knows they were throwing plenty of furniture around.) When
his father, a well-known surgeon, came home at lunchtime,
they discussed the situation. A car was watching the house so
there was no sneaking Alberto out. His father called a general
whose life he had saved in the operating room, after a guerrilla attack. The general promised to arrange everything and
called back an hour later to explain the plan.

According to the general, Alberto and his father were to
come in the next morning to fill out some forms. A routine
matter. The next day they drove downtown. The officials
questioned Alberto's father and sent him home. They needed
to ask Alberto some questions alone, they said, then they
would send him along.

When Alberto failed to return that night, his father con-
tacted the general again.

"There were problems," the general told him, "I'm sorry."

By that time Alberto had already been beaten, tortured, and thrown, blindfolded, into a cell.

In the documentary, a man looks into the camera and says with his best BBC voice, "Here behind me you see the cell where Alberto was held. This is where, every Sunday, he wrote his letters. Long letters. Love letters, if you will."

The camera pans around the little cell with its two stone benches that doubled as beds.

"Everything doubled as something else," Alberto once told a human-rights group. "Everything had to have a second reason to exist. It was the only way to survive. If they had you move a piece of furniture, you took advantage of the opportunity to pass some information to another detainee. If you fulfilled some useful function in the detention center—filing, repairing equipment—you had a better chance of surviving. Even names. Everyone had two names. The guards invented names for themselves like 'Wolf' or 'Tiger.' And they invented second names for the prisoners, too. I was *El Doctorcito*: 'Doc,' I guess you'd say."

The British filmmakers were in Groningen, shooting, for almost two weeks. During that time they interviewed Alberto in his home and in his office. They also shot footage of him walking along the canals and stopping on the little bridges, as well as tracking shots of the countryside.

"It will come out very picturesque," a cameraman named Brian told Alberto. "Groningen is a very picturesque town."

He was right on both counts.

Actually, Alberto became quite good friends with Brian during those weeks, better than with the actual director, Ian Woolridge. Brian liked to drink, he had lived in Spain, and the two of them went out to a pub almost every night.

When he was drinking, Alberto preferred to speak in Spanish, and after enough rounds Brian started speaking Spanish, too.

It was to Brian that Alberto confessed that it was, in fact, true that he had knowingly treated a *guerrillero*. He also confessed another thing. He had been with his father in the operating room when they had saved the wounded general.

"I saved lives on both sides," Alberto said.

"*Vida doble*," Brian laughed, picking up his pint of beer.

"*Vida de médico*," Alberto told him. "A doctor's life. You save whoever needs saving. My father didn't list me among the operating-room personnel because it was before I had my degree. An emergency, you see? They needed one more set of hands, so I scrubbed up."

"And the *guerrillero*?" Brian asked.

"Just like the general," he said, "I couldn't refuse to treat him."

Brian laughed. He held up his glass to the bartender to ask for another pint. "Well, we certainly don't want to put all that in the film," he said.

Alberto remembers walking home from the pub that night, seeing his reflection in the canals as he crossed the little bridges. He was drunk enough by the end of the night that he was not sure whether he had actually told Brian about the *guerrillero* and the general or had only thought of doing so. He shrugged. Brian was so far gone he probably wouldn't remember anyway.

When no one mentioned it to Alberto again, he decided he had perhaps only thought of saying something. Alberto discovered the truth when he received a letter from Ian Woolridge a year after the film came out. Ian reminded him that they hadn't tipped his hand and asked him to do a small favor.

The maze of secret detention centers in Argentina was its own universe, with its own inexplicable rules and its own strange rites. In the documentary they show the little block of cells, and the camera pans past the room where prisoners were given electric shocks.

"About four months after Alberto was sequestered, a second man was put in his cell with him," the narrator in the documentary explains.

Alberto's cellmate was a peasant named Pedro. In the guerrilla movement that Pedro belonged to, everyone had a code name. Pedro's had been Manuel.

"They'll kill me right off," Pedro kept saying in the first weeks. "I know they will. They'll kill me because I'm a *guerrillero.*"

But it became clear after a time that this was only wishful thinking on Pedro's part. Pedro was kept alive because one of the guards was amused by Pedro's squealing when they tortured him.

"*Sos muy cómico*," the guard told him one day. "You are very funny. We want to keep you around."

They became friends. Pedro told Alberto about the little village he came from and how his father had always been a socialist. He said the worst moment of his life was the night they came to his house and arrested him. "Not because they caught me," he explained. "I expected to be arrested or killed someday. But because when they led me outside, I heard a voice say, 'That's him. That's Manuel.' Then I knew someone had betrayed me."

Pedro had been in prison for about a month when he got word through the grapevine that his wife was being held in the women's building. Until then he hadn't known whether they had taken her, too.

"She's pregnant," he told Alberto one day. "We're having a

baby. I'm very worried."

In the documentary they show a photo taken in profile of Pedro's wife. She looks pregnant all right, though in fact the picture was taken years earlier on a day when a strong wind had puffed out her blouse. When Rosario's mother showed Woolridge the family pictures, he knew instantly that he wanted it for the pregnancy shot.

"Rosario was about three months pregnant when she was arrested," the voice-over narrator says. "At first the guards did not even know."

The camera follows the narrator outside onto a grassy area. A small building some forty yards away swims into view.

"The building you see before you was the women's prison," the narrator continues. "That is where Rosario was held. She had no idea where Pedro was, nor even if he was alive, until they delivered his first letter. Only then did she discover that he was being held less than a hundred yards away."

The only detainees who could write to each other were husbands and wives. The problem was that while Pedro's wife knew how to write, Pedro was almost illiterate.

One day Pedro asked Alberto a favor.

"It doesn't matter to me if you know all my intimate details," he said, "if only you will read my wife's letters to me and let me dictate my responses through you. Her name is Rosario and she is pregnant."

So on Sundays, when the prisoners were allowed to remove their blindfolds, Alberto would read Rosario's letters to Pedro in a whisper and then scribble Pedro's responses.

Alberto found himself writing things like "I sometimes think that if we survive this, Rosario, we will never complain about anything again (though I know we will)," and "My dear, do you remember that time we took a night bus from the capital to Córdoba and made love right there in the seats under a blanket?" and even "Rosario, I have discovered an eternity of love inside me and that eternity is you and the baby you are making for us."

When the two men learned through the prison grapevine (you could not put such things in a letter) that Rosario had started bleeding and had to lie all night on the floor of her cell to keep from losing the baby, Pedro was too distraught to dictate anything. That Sunday Alberto wrote the whole letter in Pedro's name. It was a long letter and it took him a couple of hours to write. "I think of you," Alberto wrote for Pedro, "and I dream of you, and I tell myself that our son (I am sure it is a boy, *¡perdoname!*) will be stronger for this and will come into life as sure and just as the cause we have fought for." Shortly before dinner Alberto read the whole letter out to Pedro. Pedro's head nodded wearily up and down.

"It is as though you knew her," he said, "as though you were her husband, too."

He hugged Alberto, and the two of them wept.

Pedro to Rosario:

Querida Rosario,

I am writing quickly today. For various reasons I could not start this letter until later than usual, please excuse me.

I am wondering how you are. I have been thinking about you nonstop for the last week—about you and the baby. How is the baby? Is he kicking yet? I remember my mother always said that it made her happy when she felt me kicking inside her, even though it hurt. She said to herself it meant she would have a strong son. Sometimes I think I have still not stopped kicking, *¿no?*

Tell me how you have been eating. For some reason our

food has improved a little lately. I don't know if this will be a regular practice or not. I know one guard who might carry some food across to the women's block, if need be. So let me know if you've noticed a change.

Oh, another thing. My doctor-cellmate, Alberto, says it is time for you to begin doing birthing exercises. Breathing intervals. You must tell me whether you already know what to do or whether you need instructions. Alberto can explain everything to me and I will explain it to you.

I am beginning again after a pause. If I want them to take this letter across to your side, I have to be done in fifteen minutes. That's what the guard just said. (He's pretty nice, though. I'm hoping he'll give me twenty minutes. My hand is a little cramped and I can't write very fast.)

I have been thinking so much about you, Rosario—about what you look like, about what you think about things. I have played a little game with myself this week. It goes like this: I think of something—anything—and then I ask myself what you would say about it. It is a mental exercise. I do this as a way of being closer to you. I can play the game with anything. Some of the things I thought of were: the poster of a soccer player I used to have in my bedroom, the way the light looks in your neighborhood just before the sun goes down, and the lousy chocolates my *abuela* always offers when you go visit her.

Listen, I must go. The guard has already banged on the door twice and is getting impatient. Besides it's getting dark and I can hardly see my writing.

Dear Rosario, take care of yourself and of your cellmate. I can hardly wait to get your letter and I will write again next week.

Besos,
Pedro

Rosario to Pedro:

Mi querido,

Your last letter was such a pleasure to receive, thank you very much.

I am doing as well as can be expected here. Don't worry about food, since some of the other women here help me out whenever they have something extra. I feel ashamed to take their food, but I am eating for two. Yes, whenever the baby moves (which he does more and more!) it makes me think of you. Pedro, I have you inside me!

You asked in one of your last letters (two weeks ago, if I am not mistaken) if I had begun thinking about a name for the baby. The answer is: yes and no. Yes, I sometimes think about names, and for about a day or two there is one that I like. But then I wake up a different morning and maybe I remember someone I once knew who had the same name—someone I couldn't stand, *¿entendés?*—and I ask myself how I could have ever considered it. So no, I have not really thought of any names. Of course, if it is a girl I would like one of her names to be Maria. And if it is a boy, we are almost obliged to put Jorge as one of his names, in honor of your father and grandfather. By the way, you too should think about names...

I'm back after a little interruption. I have been noticing recently the way the light comes in differently because of the movement of the sun. I calculate that in about three weeks, it will fall right on my face if I sit in my favorite spot in the cell. What do you think of that?

Pedro, you must tell Alberto to explain everything he knows about pregnancy and preparing for delivery, in as much detail as he can, then you must put it all into your letters. I can tell that Alberto is a very good person and I am sure he is an excellent doctor. Tell him he now has a patient by correspondence. He needs to explain about the breathing exercises—

about what exactly I need to practise doing. Also you said he mentioned that we will need to feel for the head so we know how the baby is positioned. But he needs to be more specific! When precisely? And how?

Please forgive me if I am making demands on Alberto, but he is the only doctor that has been recommended to us here (joke!). My cellmate of course pictures him as tall and handsome, but I told her he is probably short and fat.

I must end this letter here. Pedro, I miss you.

Rosario

Alberto sighs and sips the *maté*.

One of the things you learned in prison was to hoard—anything and everything—then dole it out as needed. Even thoughts. Even secrets.

Especially secrets, Alberto thinks. It becomes a habit in prison and you can't shake it afterwards. The world divides into the people you tell your secrets to and those you don't. And it further divides into the people you only tell a few secrets to and those who know them all. Over time Pedro and Alberto told each other almost all their secrets. They compared notes on their lives. Pedro always said the jail was democracy since despite their different backgrounds they were both in the same shit.

Alberto told Pedro every secret but one, and then only because he couldn't.

He looks at the woman across from him. Over the years they have grown more and more silent together. Alberto sometimes thinks that it is because making noise is so easy. The detention center was, to his surprise, a noisy place. There always seemed to be someone yelling. Outside the cells people only yelled. Guards yelled at detainees. Detainees wailed when they got shocks. Alberto sometimes thinks it takes a long time to learn how to be silent.

He passes the *maté* to her. She sips and passes it back. When the water in the gourd gets low, he pours in more hot water and stirs it. Some people put sugar in *maté*. He did that too before he was in prison, but the *maté* there never had sugar, and he got used to it. Now Alberto prefers the natural, bitter taste.

He smiles that smile. It is good to have someone who knows all your secrets.

In the documentary the camera slowly pans down one of the remaining letters. *Querida Rosario*, it begins. A voice in Spanish—Alberto's voice, in fact—begins to read. Then his voice fades and is replaced by the narrator's voice-over reading a translation of the letter as the camera slowly moves down.

Halfway down the page there is a small blank space. Then the writing begins again. The writing is cramped, almost illegible. "I tried to write poorly," Alberto says on camera in one of the interview sections. "I kept thinking, 'Write these letters in your worst prescription handwriting.'"

"Because Pedro wouldn't know how to write well?" Ian Woolridge (off camera) asks.

"Mostly because it's harder to read," Alberto answers with a little smile.

Alberto remembers that Ian was fascinated with the letters, almost feverish when they set up the shot for the film. He personally took charge of the lighting and used a lot of yellow.

"I want it to look like an old manuscript," Ian told Brian before they shot. "Like it was written by Christopher Columbus."

That night in the pub Alberto mentioned his misgivings to Brian.

"Alberto," Brian explained, "when you film, it's an effect you're after. That's what counts."

Given Ian's interest in the letters, it came as no surprise that the favor he asked was about them. A friend—"English, actually, though he has a Dutch name and lives in Amsterdam"—was putting together some sort of volume of testimonial literature.

"I told him about your letters," Ian wrote, "and he'd like to publish them."

Ian followed the letter with a call.

"Frankly, I'm not sure if he's thinking of publishing them as they are," Ian said, "or fleshing out the correspondence a little. He's a writer. Anyway I told him there were only seven. Alberto, just do us a little favor, will you? It's all for a good cause."

When he got off the phone, Alberto found himself thinking of the wounded general on the operating table, then of the *guerrillero* who showed up one day with two rounds in his abdomen. He had helped both sides.

"Alberto found love in prison," the BBC narrator says, smiling perkily into the camera. "As for Carmen, it was because of love that she ended up in jail. Or, better put: because she didn't want to face the fact that she was no longer in love."

Carmen had been so infatuated with Luis, the Peronist. That's what made her love the whole movement. She soon became disillusioned, however. But leaving the movement meant leaving Luis—as well as her job, since the Peronists had given Carmen a job as a secretary. On her way home from work each day, Carmen would think about quitting. That's what she was doing when a paramilitary squad swooped down on her one afternoon.

In the detention center Carmen thought about her family. Catholics, all of them. Her parents had always done philanthropic work. Carmen remembered Sunday afternoons from her childhood when they went into the *villas miserias*—into the poorest neighborhoods—to help feed and clothe people. Her father always said it was a scandal for a country as rich as Argentina not to feed its own. "The meek will inherit the earth, my Carmencita," he would tell her, "remember that."

But what Carmen remembered was the dark of the little one-room shacks with *chapa* walls and dirt floors, and the barefoot children who stared at her like she was a princess. Huts almost as dark as jail cells.

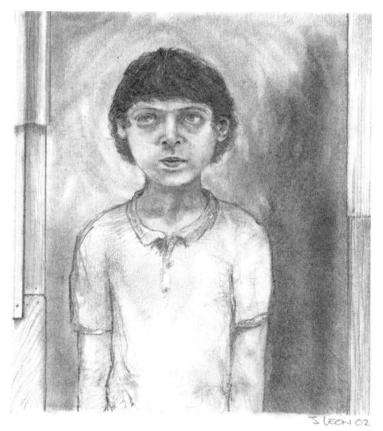

She also remembered the Catholic boarding school she had attended. One day when she was eleven she told Sister Rosa her stomach hurt. Sister Rosa handed her a sort of diaper and told her to wear it for a week. Every month they gave Carmen two diapers, and for a year and a half, until she got her period, Carmen pretended to use them, dutifully washing them out like the older girls did.

By the time she entered university, Carmen no longer believed in the priests or the pope or the good sisters. Then she met Luis.

"I'll kill that boy if he ever comes here!" her father had shouted. "Peronists are Communists!"

One day her father slapped her during an argument about Luis, so Carmen moved out of her family's house. The movement was going to be her new family. But to her surprise, she discovered the Peronists did not really care about the poor.

"*¿Te gusta el tango?*" her interrogator asked her the first time they tied her down on the metal bed. The *picana* in the guard's hand looked like a hair dryer with two loose wires. "You like tango music?"

Carmen was too scared even to lie. She was trying to figure out how she would keep from selling out her friends.

She nodded her head quickly. Yes.

The man laughed.

"You won't anymore," he said, and he turned up a cassette of tango hits before he began prodding her with the *picana*.

Carmen's great fear was that she would divulge information. In the movement they used to say that people should try to hold out for twenty-four hours—long enough for others to go into hiding. Holding out forever was too much to ask.

But to Carmen's surprise, she didn't give any names. She found she couldn't. Not even when the current they sent through her jaw made it feel like all her teeth were on fire. Not even when her nipples bled from having been burnt by the *picana*. The rage she felt at what they were doing came over her like a white sheet. The sheet didn't protect her from the pain, only from speaking.

A sheet of rage. Moreover Carmen knew where the rage came from: the Catholic church. In a strange way, Carmen became a Catholic again in prison. Not in the sense of believing, but in the sense of having a clear idea of right and wrong. She could not let herself give in to something so obviously evil, and she drew strength from the teachings instilled in her by the sisters long before.

"I was imprisoned for a cause I no longer believed in and pulled through by a faith I no longer had," she told Brian one evening when she went with Alberto to the pub. "Prisons create their own logic."

Carmen sometimes thinks of the evolution of her life as being like the children's game where you whisper a message around a room and it gradually changes. There was a funny thing that happened with a message sent around the women's cellblock. The message was that a copy of Gorky's novel *The Mother* had been allowed into the prison. By the time the word got to Carmen and Rosario it had become "Gorky's mother has been thrown in jail." One day when they were all herded into a room together, the women talked of nothing else. The *Junta* will stop at nothing! they told each other.

It wasn't until a week later that a detainee pointed out that Gorky's mother had been dead for many years. In their cells the women giggled in silence about their mistake. Carmen marveled that it had all seemed so plausible.

Ian Woolridge wanted to film Alberto walking through his old prison, but Alberto refused. Still, Alberto went with them when they filmed there. He never appears on camera but he is there, unseen.

In the detention center Alberto used to think about details. Little things: how he had dribbled a soccer ball along the street in front of his house as a kid; or how he and his friends had giggled about the wife of the grocer at the corner. He remembered family picnics up in the mountains. And little incidents he had long forgotten. His father once nearly got crushed unhitching a trailer from their car. Alberto, who couldn't have been more than seven, had known for a brief moment that his father's life was in danger. Now he worried that his father would feel guilty that he, Alberto, was in jail. Had his father telephoned the general to tell him that Alberto had been part of the team that saved the general's life?

Alberto could imagine the general's voice on the telephone: "It is out of my hands, my friend. I'm sorry."

Alberto showed the film crew where everything had been in the jails. The prisons had been abandoned, and they were able to walk right through.

In 1992, a friend wrote to say the buildings had been bulldozed. Now Alberto is glad that those dark rooms have been caught on 16mm film. That celluloid strip somehow proves it all happened, that it was not just one long nightmare. Those dark spaces haunted by Carmen's invisible image…

Alberto was useful in jail—served, that is, a purpose for his jailers. This is probably what saved him.

Once, at a human-rights meeting, a man stood up and accused Alberto of collaborating with torturers. It caused a commotion in the meeting hall. Alberto thought of the wounded general and the guerrilla fighter. He responded with the hippocratic oath, but it seemed insufficient.

The guards had stopped torturing Alberto directly. Instead they used him to revive prisoners when they passed out under the *picana*.

Was Alberto still saving lives? He hoped so.

Pedro, on the other hand, really got the treatment. Sometimes he was so weak after a session that he had to take a breath after every word when he talked.

"We hate *guerrilleros* even more than Jews," a guard named Tiburón whispered in Alberto's ear one day when he was called into the little room to attend to Pedro. "We're curious to see how much he can take."

There were times when it was hard to bring Pedro around. Alberto could see Pedro slowly weakening.

With time it got so that Pedro did not really dictate the letters to his wife but just sketched the general idea. Then Alberto would put pen to paper and craft the letter Pedro had in mind. When he got done he would read it over to Pedro if there was time and if Pedro was not too exhausted.

Alberto also mixed practical advice into a husband's concerns.

"You must practise your breathing every day," Alberto told Rosario in one letter. "Your cellmate must count seconds, and you must breathe lightly. First for thirty-second intervals, then for longer. This is for our baby."

The next letter from Rosario told Pedro, "I am practising all the exercises. I have a new cellmate who helps me. She says you have a very good doctor friend there. Her name is Carmen."

Rosario was also eating better under Carmen's watch. Rosario was in her sixth month now. "Carmen can hear the heart beating when she puts her ear to my stomach," Rosario wrote. "It is exciting and fills me with hope. I only wish you were with me for this, Pedro."

"I wish I were there, too," Alberto told her in the next letter. "But you must also try to find the head," he added at the same time. "That way we can figure out the position of

the baby. Tell Carmen to feel for it. This is very important, my
dear, as important as the love between us."

"In jail you had to look for the little spaces—the little
forgotten corners of a room or of your mind," Alberto says
straight into the camera. He is standing on a small dike, one of
the oldest in Groningen. It was his idea to film there. In the
thirteenth century the people of the area banded together for
their common good and built the first walls to keep out the
sea. "Little inattentions on the authorities' part. Tiny spaces
and errors. Little moments when you could be free."

"That's how you came up with your idea?" Ian Woolridge,
off camera, asks.

Something flits across Alberto's eyes, then it is gone. He
would have told Pedro his final secret if he had been able to.
But there was no way.

"The idea just occurred to me," Alberto says matter of
factly. "After all, I was already composing Pedro's letters."

As he sits in the café, sipping his *maté*, he thinks of those
letters—and of the ones that survived because he hid them.
Alberto chuckles about Ian Woolridge.

He remembers the telephone call from London, about a
month after he mailed the correspondence to Amsterdam:
Ian's perplexed voice on the other end.

"Alberto, is that you?"

He nodded. "Here, my friend."

"Alberto, didn't you always tell me there were only seven
letters left?"

Alberto nodded again. "That's right."

"Well then, I'm confused," Ian clipped his words. "My man
in Amsterdam says you sent him copies of nine."

Alberto smiled a little.

"I did?" Albert asked.

"He swears by it," Ian answered.

"*Probleem*," Alberto said in Dutch. "Maybe something else got mixed in," he added. "Impossible to use, then."

One Sunday, when they had their blindfolds off, Alberto told Pedro he needed to talk to him. It was serious.

"I have had an idea," he said.

Pedro nodded.

"You are my friend," Alberto told him slowly. "I think Rosario is a little bit my friend, too," he said.

"I think Rosario is a little bit your wife," Pedro said weakly, then he joked: "Please don't tell me you want to sleep with her."

Alberto smiled. But he grew serious and began again.

"Rosario is a bit my friend," he reiterated. "But I need another friend too, Pedro," Alberto said. "I need my own woman friend."

Pedro laughed outright now. Alberto realized it was the first time he had ever seen Pedro laugh.

"You've gone crazy," Pedro said. "*¡Te volviste loco, che!* Have you forgotten where you are?"

Alberto nodded slowly.

"An idea has come to me," he continued with deliberation, "*Me vino una idea.*" The way he said it, it sounded like something that had flown into their cell on wings. Then after a moment, he added, "I want to start writing letters to Carmen."

Alberto had already worked it out in his mind.

Since only husbands and wives could write each other, the sole way for him to correspond with Carmen was to tack letters to her onto the end of Pedro's letters to Rosario. Carmen would then do the same from her end. To avoid suspicion, they would have to keep using Pedro's and

Rosario's names. And the handwriting had to stay the same. On Alberto's end this did not matter because he always wrote Pedro's letters. But at the other end, Carmen would have to dictate her part of each letter to Rosario.

It took several carefully crafted letters to Rosario before she succeeded in reading between the lines. For three different weeks he tucked little hints subtly but insistently into his calm sentences—so subtly no guard would ever notice, even if he chose to read the letter. But insistently enough that sooner or later Rosario would understand.

Finally a letter came back from Rosario that mentioned, "My friend Carmen says your doctor's ideas are always good ones. She likes all his suggestions."

Alberto knew they had understood.

From then on the letters were always written in two sections. The first was between Pedro and Rosario. The second began after a little space and was between Alberto and Carmen. This went on Sunday after Sunday. Alberto patiently wrote out Pedro's letter to Rosario, then he slowly penned his continuation to Carmen. At the other end, Carmen would read over Alberto's part, substituting "Alberto" or "Carmen" every time it said "Pedro" or "Rosario." Then she would slowly dictate her response to him while Rosario scribbled it down.

Little by little Alberto-Pedro and Carmen-Rosario got to know each other.

Only Carmen knows Alberto's final and most precious secret. His most secret of secrets. At first she hated him for it, now she understands better and loves him for it. That is why she can sit in silence and sip *maté* with him, day after day, in a cold country so far from her home. She understands. He did what he had to do to survive. That's the way it was as a detainee. She forgives him, even if Rosario can't.

Alberto thinks of the day the new guard came on duty.

This was only a week after Rosario gave birth. Alberto never knew what happened to the other guard: he got transferred, probably. It was one of those things that happened in jail.

A Sunday afternoon. The new guard banged on the door of Alberto's cell.

"Letter for the *guerrillero*," he said.

Alberto sits and quietly sips his *maté* in the café. Nothing shows on his face. It is the same when he has to tell a patient that an illness is terminal.

Nothing shows. But inside Alberto is begging forgiveness.

Carmen, sitting across from him, knows he is thinking about the new guard and the letters and Pedro. She reaches for the gourd and looks into Alberto's eyes. Her look says she has long since pardoned him. Carmen believes in grace—a grace bestowed by humans. Alberto's secret is safe with her.

"Letter for the *guerrillero*," the new guard said.

Alberto tried to picture Carmen. She was dark and small. No, she was tall and almost German looking, with light skin. She had a long, pointed nose. Then she had a petite nose. She had proud shoulders that flared out like wings. She hunched over. She had a soft roundness in her belly and big flanks. She had slim hips like a boy.

Rosario wrote in one letter that if the baby turned out to be a girl ("It just might be, my darling. After all, these things are out of our control"), she wanted to name it Carmen.

"Carmen is a fine name," Alberto wrote back. And for once his many years of schooling came in handy: "It means 'song' in Latin," he told her. "Carmencita will be our little song of love."

What he didn't say was that Pedro did not see either her letter or the response Alberto wrote that week. They had taken Alberto into where they were giving Pedro electric shocks two days before, but Alberto couldn't bring him around. Alberto had tried everything: pressing Pedro's chest, breathing into his mouth, pumping his arms. Alberto ended up dragging Pedro back to their cell. Pedro was out cold until early evening when he started groaning. After that, Pedro was groggy for days.

"Sometimes I dream of you," Carmen wrote Alberto one week. "I dream that we are walking through fields near my parents' home. In my dream I have known you for a long time—for almost my whole life. You are like a brother. But in the dream I can't see your face. You are walking a little behind me. I keep thinking I should turn around and look at you, but I don't. It is sunny in the dream."

To which Alberto sent back the response, "A dream of sunshine! You must be the only detainee who dreams of sunshine! You haven't given up your hope! What I would give to see the sun with you!"

What he didn't tell her was that he was worried he might be falling in love.

"I want to live," he wrote one week. Then: "I want to live with you. What am I saying? With you? Near you? I don't know. I think about you all the time. It makes me afraid."

To which Carmen answered:

"We are all afraid. Try not to be. Think of me as I think of you. You are with me whenever you think of me."

Finally Alberto ventured forth:

"*Te quiero.* Those words we have heard all our life. This pen almost slips out of my hands as I write them. I have no business saying such things. But I can't hold myself back. So there it is: I love you."

When Rosario went into labor, they sent for Alberto. Not at first, but when it dragged on, and Rosario was making such a racket. Carmen yelled at the guards to go fetch him. "Her husband's cellmate, he's a doctor!"

"What do we care?" one of them shrugged, but he did it anyway.

Then they led Alberto across the little yard to the women's cellblock. It was a late winter day and cold, but Alberto was happy to feel the wind and see the sky, if only for a moment. A wan sun glanced over the roof of the warehouse.

When Alberto got to Rosario, the baby's head was beginning to crown and the mother was panicking. Carmen was with her, trying to talk to her.

"How long has she been having cramps?" Alberto asked.

"About five hours," Carmen answered.

"Soap and hot water," Alberto shouted at the guards. "I need soap and water!"

Two guards were standing at the doorway.

"*Esta puta*," one of them said. "This whore is having a real time!"

"Soap and water!" Alberto shouted. "And a clean towel!"

"Okay, okay, okay," the other guard answered wearily and trotted off.

What Carmen remembers is Alberto's hands. She watched his hands: first as he washed and dried them on the towel (where had the guards found a towel that was clean and folded, such a luxury?). Then as they felt around the edge of the birth opening. She marveled to see before her now the fingers that had penned so many letters. She observed the methodical way his hands went to work. She remembered how in her province the farmers would sometimes reach up right into the birth canal to pull out a baby calf. She thought for a second Alberto might do the same. She was also amazed to discover that the hair on his arms was thick and black and spilled over his knuckles like some kind of wild goat's.

She hadn't expected that.

As for Alberto, he was so preoccupied with the birth that it hardly registered that the woman beside him was Carmen. He both knew it and didn't know it. At that moment Carmen was just another nurse.

Rosario had been in labor for about seven hours when the baby finally came. The cramps were coming one right after another.

Carmen was holding Rosario's hand, checking her pulse, and talking her through the pain.

The cramps came at thirty-second intervals now: violent, burning, terrifying.

"Pedro! Pedro!" Rosario sometimes panted as she caught her breath between cramps.

"Pedro will be here soon," Alberto answered mechanically. He had been through many birthings among the mountain peasants. No matter what a woman cried out, you always agreed.

The head cleared now. Alberto could see part of a squashed nose. He knew this was the moment. It was now or never.

"Push, Rosario!" he shouted. His voice was harsh, almost desperate. "¡Empujalo! You must push, dammit!"

Rosario pushed with all her might.

"¡Más fuerte!" Alberto cried. "Bear down on it! Rosario!"

Rosario cried out. "I can't!"

Carmen held Rosario's hands, but her head lashed about.

"Si, ¡podés!" Alberto ordered. "Don't let up!"

"Push, Rosario!" Carmen prayed.

And then suddenly there it was—a birth as smooth and rich as butter: a baby.

The head swam up between her legs like an amphibious being from another world. Then the shoulders began to show, pinched and vulnerable.

Alberto reached in with a finger to make sure the umbilical cord was not getting crushed.

"Keep pushing!" he muttered.

"Push!" Carmen begged beside him. "Push, Rosario!" Alberto saw her cross herself. Then he felt her hands gripping his arm.

"She did it!" Carmen was crying. "She did it!"

"Alberto, look!" Carmen said as the baby slipped out. For a second Alberto held the slippery body, its feet dangling beside it like lifeless limbs. "Is it alive?"

The guards had gotten bored and left.

Just then the mouth opened and a funny little screech came out. The baby's hands made gripping motions and one wrist seemed to want to paw its face. The baby gave a squeaky cry again.

Rosario's belly convulsed: half laugh, half cry.

"A boy," Carmen told her. "Here, Rosario. *Tomalo en tus brazos.* Take your son."

They laid the baby on Rosario's belly. Alberto's hands were at the entrance to the birth canal, waiting for the placenta.

"Nurse him," Alberto suggested gently, and with one hand he kneaded Rosario's stomach while the other brought the placenta out.

When the baby began to suck, Alberto felt Rosario's stomach tighten. He heaved a sigh of relief. The cervix was closing. A miracle—there was no tearing. No tearing, no hemorrhaging.

"A clean knife!" Alberto shouted into the hallway. "I need a clean knife."

"What for?" one of the guards called in a bored voice. "You think we give knives to prisoners?"

"To cut the cord," Alberto said. "Just bring it."

"*Está bien*," the guard said in the same tone, "okay, okay."

"Christ," his companion muttered, "why not just let the bitch die?"

Soon the guard stood over Alberto as he cut the cord. Alberto handed the knife back to the guard as though to an operating-room attendant. Alberto knotted the stub.

Carmen and Rosario had managed to wash some cloth and keep it clean for swaddling. A section torn from a sheet. As Alberto rolled the baby into the cloth in Carmen's hands he looked at her for the first time.

When he got back to his own cell Alberto realized that Carmen had blue eyes.

"*¿Qué va a pasar con el nene?*" he asked her. "What's happening with the baby?"

After all, the military often stole newborn children.

"They say she can keep it," Carmen tried to sound reassuring. "It's all right."

Fifteen minutes later they were leading Alberto back to the men's building. The sun had disappeared entirely, though whether it had actually gone down behind the shed or was just obscured by clouds, Alberto didn't know. He also noted briefly that the wind had died down.

Then they were in the dark building and the guards blindfolded him and bound his wrists again. A moment later they had pushed him into his cell. Alberto settled himself against the wall. After the steps of the guards retreated, he began to whisper.

"A boy, Pedro," he said. "Think of it! *Un varón*, healthy and crying. I had him in my hands. He must be over two kilos. Big enough to pull through fine." He paused. "And Rosario's doing well."

He waited.

"Pedro, dammit, are you listening?" he finally whispered.

For an awful moment he thought Pedro might be passed out.

"Pedro!" he said in a harsh whisper.

Then suddenly Alberto knew. Even as he began to pat around the cell he knew. Wouldn't that be just like them—?

"*¡Qué boludos!*" Alberto muttered to himself.

After he had felt all the way around the cell—it didn't take very long—he started again just to make sure. He also methodically covered the open space of the floor.

By the time Alberto was done he knew that unless Pedro had shrunk to the size of an ant, he was not there.

"The motherfuckers!" he said to himself, and for a second he wasn't sure whether he was more in danger of crying or of screaming.

That night he had nightmares.

The next morning Alberto racked his brain to remember what day of the week it was. Friday? Saturday? It was a bad sign if he didn't know.

The time was interminable, he couldn't stand it. Alberto thought of the tadpole-like body he had lifted out of Rosario. He tried to remember what Carmen looked like, but he could recall only her eyes. Why hadn't he looked at her body, too? Alberto had the impression of a thin woman with strong legs. She had sat on her heels almost the whole time she attended to Rosario.

But most of all Alberto thought about Pedro. He knew what it meant when a prisoner didn't show up for a whole day.

Around midday Alberto realized it was Sunday because someone put a radio in the corridor outside the cells so the prisoners could listen to a soccer game. The guards did that sometimes.

Late in the afternoon he heard someone outside his door. It opened.

"*Vamos*," a voice said. It was Tiburón. "We need your help. Guy might be dead, we're not sure."

They undid his blindfold and unshackled his hands.

Alberto was expecting the worst.

But it wasn't Pedro. Instead it was some thin fellow who looked Bolivian. He was naked and lying on his stomach on a metal table, with his head hanging over the edge.

"Yeah," Alberto said before he even got to him, "he's dead all right."

"That's what we thought," Tiburón said as he led Alberto back to his cell.

No letter that day.

Alberto was desperate to know how Rosario was faring. He wondered what had happened with the baby. He thought he would go crazy.

He had never wanted so much to write a letter in his life.

After they got their blindfolds off, he asked to go to the john. There was another guy in the urinal.

"Where's Pedro?" Alberto asked while the guard was busy lighting a cigarette.

"*No tengo idea*," the man said, shaking the last drop off his penis.

"If you see him, tell him he had a son," Alberto told him.

"Sure thing," the prisoner said.

Then Alberto was back in the dark cell, trying to piece it all together. The important thing was to keep his thoughts clear.

But he couldn't. He was panicking. They had figured it out, he told himself. They were doing all this on purpose. This was part of the torture. Somehow they had caught on. In a cold sweat he remembered he had torn off and saved two small sections from Carmen's part of a letter. They had probably searched his cell one day and found them. Maybe they already knew everything before they took him across for the birth. They had probably guffawed about his being in love.

If so, Carmen and Rosario were in danger now, and so was the baby. As for Pedro, it was almost certainly too late.

Alberto reached for the chink near the head of his cement bed where he had tucked the two slips of paper. It didn't look like anyone had been there. To be on the safe side he pulled the bits of paper out, balled them up as small as he could, and shoved them up his nostrils. If you got them in deep enough the guards couldn't see them during a body search, not even with a flashlight.

By Monday Alberto knew he would never hear from Rosario and Carmen again. He had never thought about the fact that without Pedro he would lose all contact with Carmen.

What the hell, had he thought it would go on forever? Had he been assuming (he asked himself) they would keep Pedro alive just so Alberto could go on writing to Carmen? That kind of thinking was dangerous on the inside.

He told himself that in order to survive he had to forget about Rosario and Carmen. It had to be as if Carmen had never existed. No more or less than all the other women in the adjacent building—the ones he had never known. Now he needed to forget Rosario and Carmen. Forget them entirely.

"Forget her," he whispered to himself out loud, to see what the thought sounded like. "Forget Carmen."

This went on for days.

"Make them be dead for you," he whispered to himself under his blindfold. "They never existed." It was a practical decision.

"You have to survive," he told himself. "You have survived this far. Survive!"

Then the following Sunday a new guard rapped on the door. It was a voice Alberto had never heard before.

"Letter for the *guerrillero*," the guard said. That's what they always called Pedro. "From his wife."

Alberto thought quickly. The tiny opening in their door filled briefly with light.

"I'll take it," he snapped.

The guard slipped the letter through.

As Alberto hoped, the same guard was on duty the following Sunday. They again exchanged letters through the slit in the door. "For the *guerrillero*," the guard said.

"For my wife, Rosario," Alberto said, "in the other building."

The new guard never suspected a thing.

"*Querida Rosario*," the letter began, "Alberto told me the wonderful news as soon as he arrived back here last Sunday! A boy! A new life! Oh, Rosario, this is the start of our future…!"

Alberto had begun to write a dead man's letters.

Further down the page there was a little blank space, then the writing began again:

"We paused to eat, please excuse me. Oh, Rosario, I can think of nothing else but you! The time we had together went by so fast! Will we see each other again?"

But *Rosario* here meant *Carmen. Carmen, ¡Carmen!*

One letter led to another. And another.

"What am I doing?" Alberto asked himself each week as he began to write in Pedro's name. "I must stop! I must make this my last letter."

But each Sunday he wrote a new one.

After all, Rosario needed the letters, he told himself. "She needs to believe," he whispered into the air of the cell, to see how it sounded.

Sometimes he half-convinced himself he would tell her the truth soon. "I will find a way," he would promise to the empty cell, "once I am absolutely sure."

But he was already absolutely sure.

"Besides, Rosario is not ready to know yet."

Right now she needed to be strong for her son, he decided, and she needed Pedro's letters to be strong.

Alberto sat in the dark of his cell, writing. From his conversations with Pedro, he knew the details of Rosario's whole life. He pictured her native village in his mind. He knew what the one-room hut where her family lived looked like. He knew where the public fountain was in the village, and the chapel where her mother went to pray for Rosario every day. He saw Father José consoling Rosario's father in the street, and the questioning face of Rosario's little brother Guillermo.

Alberto had already been Pedro so many times. He could become Pedro for a little longer.

I must keep writing Rosario, he told himself. I must not let her down.

But all the while, Alberto knew this was a lie. Alone in his cell, he cursed himself for what he was doing.

"Pedro, don't be angry," he sometimes whispered to the walls, "please try to understand."

He swore again and again that he would write no more letters. But every time Alberto thought of losing contact with Carmen, he panicked. Come Sunday he wrote again.

"Forgive me, Pedro," he prayed in his dark cell. "Forgive me for keeping you alive like this."

Querida Rosario,

I awoke this morning with your image in my head. For some reason I spoke your name—as though it had been there in my mouth all night. Perhaps I thought I was with you? Perhaps I had been dreaming?

Then I thought of our son, Rosario. *¡Nuestro hijo!* It is wonderful to pronounce those words!

Rosario, whatever name you decide on is fine with me. In your last letter you suggested "Alberto Jorge." Maybe "Jorge Alberto" would be better, no? I know Alberto will feel flattered in either event, and my father will be proud to have his name first, not second.

I must confess I am tired today. I have felt a little weak recently. But I am overjoyed to know that a life we have made is laughing and crying. Soon he will be crawling and walking. I look forward to the day when we will see him running through those narrow streets...

Because I was tired, I took a little rest. Now I feel refreshed. Rosario, Alberto tells me that Carmen was a wonderful nurse during the birth. If she ever needs a job, he says, he will be more than willing to take her on as his assistant.

It is already late afternoon here, and in a little while I need to send this letter. I imagine your cell and the two of you with the baby. It is as though I have been there, I have such a clear picture of it all. What I would give to have a couple hours with you! Perhaps one day we will get out of here and we will spend hours, weeks, years together. Stranger things have happened.

Please write. Your letters are like a secret tunnel, a conduit to another world. They keep me alive.

I love you.
Pedro

After Alberto got out of jail, it took him six months to find Carmen, and all the while he was afraid he might discover the worst. He got in touch with everyone he knew who might have contacts among Peronists.

One Friday afternoon, he got a call at his work. It was a friend of a friend but he didn't give a name.

"You the guy looking for Carmen?" the voice asked.

"Maybe," Alberto answered guardedly. He had the suspicion that he might be talking to someone in uniform.

"Grab a piece of paper. I'll give you an address."

Alberto wrote her that weekend. He was not sure just what to write. How was she? Had she heard from Rosario? Did she have any news about the boy?

He was skirting the issue, he knew. Finally he decided to plunge.

"I will be blunt," he wrote. "I have to go to Buenos Aires next month. Do you want to meet there? Write me and let me know. *Un abrazo fuerte*, Alberto."

The truth was that Alberto didn't have to go to the capital at all, but he would go if Carmen did.

Two weeks later he got back her letter. She proposed a well-known café.

"Give me a date and a time, and I will be there."

The café where they met was an old one near the obelisk. It had been a gathering place for writers in the 1920s and the decor hadn't changed, except now they played jazz in the background.

When Alberto got to the café, Carmen was already waiting for him. Or rather, when Alberto got there for the second time. He had in fact arrived fifteen minutes early, but when he saw she wasn't there he went a block away, had a quick cognac, and came back.

Carmen was facing the door and she stood up at the little round table the second he came in.

Since he didn't know just what to do, Alberto both shook her hand and kissed her on the cheek.

He had only a vague image of what Carmen had looked like. For a fleeting second he thought someone might have been sent in her place.

"*Se te ve muy bien*," he told her. "You look great."

"So do you."

An elderly man in a starched white shirt took their order.

"*Café con leche* for the man, tea for the lady," the old waiter said, repeating what they told him.

"Do you want something to eat? A pastry?" Alberto asked as the waiter shuffled off.

Carmen shook her head no.

Just then Alberto remembered he had flowers.

"These are for you," he said.

The café turns up in Ian Woolridge's film. Alberto agreed to appear in that portion of the film.

"This is the very spot where they met after they were released," the narrator says as the camera pans. Alberto is sitting at a table. The camera zooms in.

"They met again and decided to marry."

When Alberto's face fills the whole frame, he begins speaking.

"It was a difficult conversation," Alberto explains in heavily accented English. "We knew we had saved each other's life through the letters. But the real question was whether there was sufficient reason to stay together once we were out of jail. We spent a weekend discussing it, and finally decided to make a try."

That was ten years ago.

Their order came and for a few moments they were busy with cream and sugar and lemon. Alberto found himself listening to the sound of the spoons scraping the inside of their cups as they stirred. It occurred to him that what he really wanted was a good *maté*.

"Rosario is well," Carmen said at last. "So is the baby, by the way. I saw them once."

"They actually let the family have it?"

Carmen nodded.

"They got a call one day that said to expect a visit. Then a man dressed in civilian clothes dropped off the baby as though he were delivering a package. Who can explain? Incidentally, I've been made godmother."

"Congratulations," Alberto smiled. "When did Rosario get out?"

"Almost the same time I did. She says they cleared us out because a human-rights group was coming. That's what someone told her."

Alberto shrugged. Carmen took a sip of her tea.

"I guess you know about Pedro," he said at last.

Carmen stopped. She set down her cup and laid her hand beside it. Her forearm was slender, with light hair like long grass.

"What about Pedro?" she asked in almost a whisper. "What do you know?"

Oh God, Alberto thought. He sighed deeply.

Alberto told Carmen his secret. He explained as briefly as possible.

A minute or two later it was all over.

After another phone call from Britain, Alberto agreed to drive down to Amsterdam and meet with Ian's friend. His name was David te Riele.

They had lunch at an Indonesian restaurant near Water-looplein. When the plates had been cleared away and the bill paid, David brought out the Xeroxed letters. It was mid-afternoon and the restaurant was almost deserted. David pulled one out of the folder.

"This letter is my favorite," he said. "This is the one I want to put at the front of the book."

Alberto began to laugh.

"What's so funny?" David asked.

Alberto had the funny feeling of being filmed or of being in a scene from a play. He could not stop laughing. It was as though the camera was drawing back suddenly, and he and David were becoming smaller and smaller. Then the restaurant. Then Waterlooplein. Then all of Amsterdam.

"I don't get it," David said, half question.

"There's nothing to get," Alberto told him. "Except the letter is bogus."

"What are you talking about?" David said.

But Alberto was already scooping up the folder and charging for the door.

"Wait a second!" David called.

"Just tell yourself the letters are all bogus," Alberto shot over his shoulder as he pushed through the door. "It's all fake."

Alberto thought Carmen might hate him. Hate him forever.

But no. She was furious, furious most of all when he tried to suggest he had done it for Rosario's sake.

"You did it because you had to survive," Carmen said without looking at him. "I understand that. But don't expect Rosario to. She still hopes against hope to find Pedro."

That was when Alberto knew his secret was safe with her.

"Now tell me how *you* got out," Carmen said.

The mock execution. Alberto told her the whole story.

It happened like this:

It was the end of the month.

One afternoon they loaded Alberto and about fifteen other prisoners into a lorry. They drove them for a couple hours—into the mountains, you could tell from the twisting roads. Finally they stopped on a deserted ridge.

The soldiers had the detainees dig a long trench. It was early evening and the sun was going down. The soldiers walked around the perimeter, smoking and joking. When they were satisfied with the work, they collected the shovels, then tied the men's hands behind their backs.

It was dark by the time they lined the men up in front of the ditch. They had them get on their knees. One soldier stood in front of each prisoner. They stuck what seemed like a cigarette in each man's mouth. It was dark so it was hard to tell.

"This is it," the platoon leader told them. "This is it, you sons of bitches."

Each soldier took his pistol out of his holster. Alberto remembers that he could hardly see the soldier in front of him.

Then there was a little pop and something flashed.

Alberto fell back into the ditch.

"I thought I was dead," he told Carmen. "I must have lain there for five minutes. The whole time I was thinking, 'This is what it's like to be dead.'"

He spread his hands flat on the table.

"They had put some kind of little explosive in our mouths. Then they kicked us in the chest and it made them go off."

The café was filling up around them. People getting off work. People on their way to movies. People having a drink before dinner.

"And?" Carmen asked.

"I heard one of the guards laughing," Alberto said. "I knew if a guard was laughing, I had to still be alive."

Then the soldiers were climbing in the lorry.

"Have a nice time, you sons of bitches," one of them called as they drove off.

When he got back to Groningen, Alberto refused to take Ian Woolridge's calls. Finally Ian wrote a letter.

Carmen called Alberto at the office to tell him.

"Bring it to the café this afternoon," he said.

When they were settled by the window in *Om de hoek*, Alberto opened the letter. From his chair he could see one of the bridges where they had filmed.

The letter was poised between coaxing and threatening.

It said these things: "We all need each other... We need to work together, otherwise they win... David is a highly respected... You'll lose your credibility in the human-rights..."

Alberto sipped the bitter *maté* as he read. Then he handed the letter across to Carmen.

Carmen read it, too, and reached for the gourd.

Alberto passed it to her. He sat looking out over the canal.

"Maybe you should just let them have the letters," she said. "After all, no one will ever know?"

Alberto lay there all night without moving. He couldn't move.

"The funny thing," Alberto explains in the film, "is that none of us moved. Fifteen prisoners. All night, there in the ditch. Without moving."

In the morning they crawled out. They had no idea where they were.

"We started walking," Alberto explains. "We walked until we came to a road. The day got warm and we took off our shirts."

From passing farmers they found out they were in Córdoba province. It slowly dawned on them they had been set free.

Were the soldiers supposed to have killed them? No one knew.

The group began to break up. They flagged down passing trucks and asked them where they were headed. The men climbed aboard the trucks according to where they lived.

The guy who gave Alberto a ride for several hundred kilometers was a fat, jolly fellow who sang a lot. The first thing he did when Alberto climbed in was hand him the steaming gourd propped against him on the seat.

"Have some *maté?*" he asked. "I just made it."

When he let Alberto out, he gave him money for a bus.

"Stay out of trouble, *¡pibe!*" he called as he drove off.

The Last Pages

A. H. HELLER
AUCTIONEER

Laceyville, Pa.   Phone 869-3621

NAME OF ARTICLE	Amount Dollars	Collected Cents	TO WHOM SOLD	PD.
Rollers		3 00	Wickizer	✓
Brushes		2 50	Arthur Ely	✓
Brushes		1 75		X
texture brush		25		X
Brushes		2 50	John Perry	✓
Brushes		2 25	Treiber	✓
tea pot		25		✓
Box of groceries		2 00	Homer Dexter	X
Bath scales		2 75		X
lunch box		1 25		X
Groceries		2 00	Ruth Moscrip	✓
double boiler		2 00	Ruth Moscrip	✓
aspirin tablets		1 50		✓
umbrella		50		X
Pan of misc		1 25	Steve Jennings	✓
alarm clock		1 50	Homer Dexter	✓
elec clock		2 75	Wm Birbeau	✓
table lighter		50	Norman Moser	✓
Box of dishes		1 00	Wickizer	✓
coffee grinder		2 00	D. Herman	X
Barometer		1 50		
German dish + basket		2 00	Anne Brown	✓
Steam iron		4 00		X
kitchen ware		75	Homer Dexter	✓
greaseless fry pan		2 25	Chas. Young	✓
Toaster		1 00	Annabelle Vough	✓

TED MORRISSEY

*W*hen I met my wife, Jane, she was engaged to a rich kid in his second year at a prestigious Chicago law school. For some reason she gave up the palatial house, the BMW, and the country club for the modest existence of marrying a teacher and writer—and that, as Frost observed, "has made all the difference." Had Jane chosen differently I might have ended up something like my title character in "Fische Stories." I didn't see the parallel when I was writing my story; I only realize it now as I type this note. My oldest son Zack took this photograph; his younger brothers are Ethan and Spenser, who share, among many other things, the same birthday.

*T*echnical breakthroughs, emotional breakthroughs. They don't mean a thing if there isn't a spark. My son, Isaiah, can serve that function for me. When I tally my good fortune, he's at the top.

DAWN KARIMA PETTIGREW

Eating the Scroll

Multitudes of people crying,
Asking for manna and pleading for quail,
Shouting, reaching, pushing, shoving,
Salt and oil, flour and lard,
Eating is everything, pass your basket,
Sit quiet, He'll give us loaves and fishes.

from *The Way We Make Sense*

LAURENCE DE LOOZE

One lost weekend in Louisville, Kentucky, my friend Maria del Carmen, to whom "Correspondence" is dedicated, told me in detail about her incarceration as a political prisoner in Argentina in the 1970s. When I asked her if I could "use" her story, she said yes immediately.

I wove Maria del Carmen's story together with two others my wife Rosa, also Argentinian, told me: one was about a doctor friend of hers who was sequestered, and the other was the story of a clandestine correspondence. Standing in the kitchen one day, Rosa also proposed a key twist in the plot. Did she suspect at the time that I was at an impasse with the story?

I wanted virtually every aspect of this tale to be riddled with contradictions. I wanted each person and each thing to be a little tainted (the only exception is the character Carmen). After I finished writing the story, it sat on my desk for five years while I tried to decide what to do next. I just wasn't sure I could publish it.

By the way, Rosa tells me she said in the beginning that the letter-writing couple was Lucy and her boyfriend; but I've always thought she told me initially that the couple ended up in Switzerland or Sweden. Must have been a different story. Rosa accuses me of having a *memoria de ormiga* ("ant's memory"), and, as it turns out, she's right!

I met Whitney Lunsford, my wife, in Scotland in 1997. In early November, along with our friend Jeremy Dean, we drove through the Scottish Highlands. It seemed like a good idea at the time—winter hadn't hit yet, and the hills were a beautiful silver-yellow color, under a silver sky.

On a narrow, one-lane highway north of Inverness, we encountered a maniacal trucker who forced us over the edge of the road and into a ditch.

Help, however, was soon on the way.

I'm on the far right.

JO-ANN GRAZIANO

*T*hat summer I salted a slug, purely by accident. I had been scrubbing the make- shift shower outside my parents' beach house and the thing must have slid up behind me. "Cool," my son Sean said, pointing it out withering in the bleach. I cringed, remembering the box of Morton's my brother would carry out to my grandmother's garden in late August. I imagined the girl in the yellow raincoat grinning like me under her umbrella as we dumped merciless amounts of sodium in the name of hygiene, science, and fun.

I washed the slug down the drain and escorted Sean to the garage. We climbed over fishing poles, pots and pans, board games. It seemed hopeless to caution Sean not to disturb things. I told him to be careful and left him to his archaeology. On the way out, I spotted my grandmother's old mayonnaise jar full of buttons. My mother, setting out a jug of peaches and wine, had already launched another of those stories she re-plays like broken records. I held out the jar. "Look what I found." I unscrewed the lid and caught the scent of my grandmother's living room from some fifteen years ago. I stuck my nose in, let my mother take a whiff, and then recapped it quickly. My mother had stopped talking.

I walked along the concrete back to the garage. "Look out, a slug." Run, I almost said, go get the salt box, but then thought better of it.

188

JENNY A. BURKHOLDER

This photo, taken by my grandfather, is of my grandmother, my mother (the small one on the left), and my aunt. I love this photo because I imagine myself as part of a long line of women, firmly affixed to the earth as if we were exquisite angels glued to a dashboard.

AARON TILLMAN

The story "The Great Salt Lake Desert" was inspired by the move—from Brooklyn to San Francisco—that my wife, Shira (beside me in this photograph), and I made almost two years ago. The truth is that she wasn't my wife at the time, and, as a semi-employed aspiring romantic, I decided that driving across country with all of my worldly possessions, not to mention two restless cats, was the best way to prove myself. Who needs sanity, anyway?

PAST CONTRIBUTING AUTHORS AND ARTISTS
Many of issues 1 through 42 are available for eleven dollars each.

Robert A. Abel • Linsey Abrams • Steve Adams • Susan Alenick • Rosemary Altea • Julia Alvarez • Brian Ames • A. Manette Ansay • Margaret Atwood • Kevin Bacon • Aida Baker • Russell Banks • Brad Barkley • Kyle Ann Bates • Richard Bausch • Robert Bausch • Charles Baxter • Ann Beattie • Barbara Bechtold • Cathie Beck • Jeff Becker • Janet Belding • Sallie Bingham • Kristen Birchett • Melanie Bishop • James Carlos Blake • Corinne Demas Bliss • Valerie Block • Joan Bohorfoush • Harold Brodkey • Danit Brown • Kurt McGinnis Brown • Paul Brownfield • Judy Budnitz • Christopher Bundy • Evan Burton • Michael Byers • Christine Byl • Gerard Byrne • Jack Cady • Annie Callan • Kevin Canty • Peter Carey • Ron Carlson • H. G. Carroll • Brian Champeau • Vikram Chandra • Mike Chasar • Robert Chibka • Carolyn Chute • George Makana Clark • Dennis Clemmens • Aaron Cohen • Robert Cohen • Evan S. Connell • Ellen Cooney • Rand Richards Cooper • Rita D. Costello • Wendy Counsil • William J. Cyr • Tristan Davies • Toi Derricotte • Janet Desaulniers • Tiziana di Marina • Junot Díaz • Stephen Dixon • Matthew Doherty • Michael Dorris • Siobhan Dowd • Eugenie Doyle • Tiffany Drever • Andre Dubus • Andre Dubus III • Wayne Dyer • Ron Egatz • Barbara Eiswerth • Mary Ellis • Susan Engberg • Lin Enger • James English • Tony Eprile • Louise Erdrich • Zoë Evamy • Nomi Eve • Edward Falco • Merrill Feitell • J.M. Ferguson, Jr. • Lisa Fetchko • Susan Fox • Michael Frank • Pete Fromm • Daniel Gabriel • Ernest Gaines • Tess Gallagher • Louis Gallo • Kent Gardien • Ellen Gilchrist • Mary Gordon • Peter Gordon • Elizabeth Graver • Andrew Sean Greer • Gail Greiner • John Griesemer • Paul Griner • Patricia Hampl • Christian Hansen • Elizabeth Logan Harris • Marina Harris • Erin Hart • Kent Haruf • Daniel Hayes • David Haynes • Daniel Hecht • Ursula Hegi • Amy Hempel • Andee Hochman • Alice Hoffman • Jack Holland • Noy Holland • Lucy Honig • Ann Hood • Linda Hornbuckle • David Huddle • Siri Hustvedt • Stewart David Ikeda • Lawson Fusao Inada • Elizabeth Inness-Brown • Debra Innocenti • Bruce Jacobson • Andrea Jeyaveeran • Charles Johnson • Leslie Johnson • Wayne Johnson • Thom Jones • Tom Miller Juvik • Cyril Jones-Kellet • Elizabeth Judd • Jiri Kajanë • Hester Kaplan • Wayne Karlin • Tom Kealey • Andrea King Kelly • Thomas E. Kennedy • Tim Keppel • Jamaica Kincaid • Lily King • Maina wa Kinyatti • Carolyn Kizer • Carrie Knowles • David Koon • Karen Kovacik • Jake Kreilkamp • Marilyn Krysl • Frances Kuffel • Anatoly Kurchatkin • Victoria Lancelotta • Jennifer Levasseur • Doug Lawson • Don Lee • Peter Lefcourt • Jon Leon • Doris Lessing • Debra Levy • Janice Levy • Christine Liotta • Rosina Lippi-Green • David Long • Nathan Long • Salvatore Diego Lopez • Melissa Lowver • William Luvaas • Richard Lyons • Bruce Machart • Jeff MacNelly • R. Kevin Maler • George Manner • Jana Martin • Lee Martin • Alice Mattison • Jane McCafferty • Judith McClain • Cammie McGovern • Eileen McGuire • Susan McInnis • Gregory McNamee • Jenny Drake McPhee • Amalia Melis • Frank Michel • Nancy Middleton • Alyce Miller • Katherine Min • Mary McGarry Morris • Mary Morrissy • Bernard Mulligan • Abdelrahman Munif • Manuel Muñoz • Karen Munro • Kent Nelson • Sigrid Nunez • Ron Nyren • Joyce Carol Oates • Tim O'Brien • Vana O'Brien • Mary O'Dell • Chris Offutt • Laura Oliver • Felicia Olivera • Stewart O'Nan • Elizabeth Oness • Karen Outen • Mary Overton • Patricia Page • Ann Pancake • Peter Parsons • Roy Parvin • Karenmary Penn • Susan Perabo • Constance Pierce • Steven Polansky • John Prendergast • Jessica Printz • E. Annie Proulx • Kevin Rabalais • Jonathan Raban • George Rabasa • Margo Rabb • Mark Rader • Paul Rawlins • Nancy Reisman • Linda Reynolds • Kurt Rheinheimer • Carol Roh-Spaulding • Anne Rice • Michelle Richmond • Alberto Ríos • Roxana Robinson • Paulette Roeske • Stan Rogal • Frank Ronan • Elizabeth Rosen • Janice Rosenberg • Jane Rosenzweig • Karen Sagstetter • Kiran Kaur Saini • Mark Salzman • Carl Schaffer • Libby Schmais • Natalie Schoen • Jim Schumock • Lynn Sharon Schwartz • Barbara Scot • Amy Selwyn • Catherine Seto • Bob Shacochis • Evelyn Sharenov • Sally Shivnan • Ami Silber • Al Sim • George Singleton • Floyd Skloot • Brian Slattery • Roland Sodowsky • R. Clifton Spargo • Gregory Spatz • Brent Spencer • L.M. Spencer • Lara Stapleton • Barbara Stevens • John Stinson • George Stolz • William Styron • Karen Swenson • Liz Szabla • Lois Taylor • Paul Theroux • Abigail Thomas • Randolph Thomas • Joyce Thompson • Patrick Tierney • Andrew Toos • Patricia Traxler • Jessica Treadway • Rob Trucks • Kathryn Trueblood • Carol Turner • Christine Turner • Kathleen Tyau • Michael Upchurch • Lee Upton • Gerard Varni • A. J. Verdelle • Daniel Villasenor • Sergio Gabriel Waisman • Daniel Wallace • Ren Wanding • Mary Yukari Waters • Jamie Weisman • Lance Weller • Ed Weyhing • Joan Wickersham • Lex Williford • Gary Wilson • Robin Winick • Terry Wolverton • Monica Wood • Christopher Woods • wormser • Celia Wren • Calvin Wright • Brennen Wysong • Jane Zwinger

Erin and Theodore, 1990

Coming soon:

When we were finished eating, we stiffly slid off the upholstered dining-room chairs and tottered away like the overstuffed munchkins from *The Wizard of Oz*, full of our grandmother's rare expression of love.

from "A Dirty Woman" by Mary Rellindes Ellis

She was from the generation of women who kept Kleenex tucked into the wrists or pockets of all their clothing, sad, lumpy corsages, as if they were grimly practical about the eventuality of tears, and she extracted some tissue now from her robe and began to cry.

from "The Glass Eaters" by Katherine Vaz

He watched his breath make clouds of vapor in the freezing air, then he slapped at it with his hand, stirring up the natural swirls into a chaotic pattern. "Get away!" he said out loud, then looked around to see if anyone had heard him. But of course no one had.

from "Gone Fishing" by Daryl Siegel

In Southern Indiana they have to tuck their cornfields away between hills and dales, and they have caves, and a river that goes underground for twenty miles, called the Lost River. They have ups and downs and unders and overs and would never allow seventy-mile stretches of nothing-but-corn the way they do up north.

from "My Town" by Scott Southwick